CABIN EIGHT

A HIGH-STAKES PSYCHOLOGICAL CONSPIRACY THRILLER

THE MILLERSVILLE SERIES
BOOK 3

SUSAN SPECHT ORAM

SOS COMMUNICATIONS LLC

Published by SOS Communications LLC in 2023

www.susanspechtoram.com

First Edition

Cover design by Best Page Forward

ISBN: 979-8-9870410-4-8 (paperback)

ISBN: 979-8-9870410-5-5 (e-book)

❀ Created with Vellum

NO OPEN FLAMES

I strike a match in a motel room in the mountains and wrinkle my nose at the smell of sulfur. Lighting a candle on the windowsill, I glance at a notice posted on the back of the door listing a bunch of rules. No open flames. Quiet time is ten p.m. until eight a.m. Wash the dishes before you leave, or you'll be charged for each dirty pan.

I shrug. I won't start a fire or make noise. I'm a house cleaner by profession, and I'll tidy up after myself.

Coming here was my mother's idea. She owns the company I work for, Diggs House Cleaning. Signs on our cars say: "We dig you. We'll leave your place spotless."

Last week, my mom said, "Miranda, you need to get out of the city. Take two days off with pay and write about what's bothering you. Burn the pages in the motel room. The ritual will help you forget what you saw."

It's been months since I've gone out of town, so I accepted her offer and gave her a hug.

Now, at the Old West themed motel where I'm staying in on the second floor, someone slams a car door. A woman about my age, in her mid-twenties, glances up and stops, studying my face. Her gaze makes me feel exposed, so I pull the curtains together, closer to the candle.

I open a diary to where I bared my soul about an incident that took place when I was twelve years old. It happened years ago, but it's fresh in my mind. I tug on a hank of my long hair. I should've saved her.

Grasping three pages in the diary, I rip them out and hold them to the candle's flickering flame.

I nod as the paper ignites. I'll have a fresh start after this. My mother was right.

Fire dances down the paper, singing my fingers.

I drop what's left of the pages and yelp, jumping back.

The fabric curtains smolder and catch fire with a crackle.

I rip the curtains off the rod and stomp on the fabric. The flames burn my ankles and tennis shoes, giving off a melting plastic smell.

I run to the bathtub, turn on the water and wet a towel.

Racing back to the curtains, I throw a wet towel over the fire to drown my mistake.

By then, it's too late.

A decorative cluster of pinecones I'd carried in after a hike burst into flames.

Fire licks the wood-paneled walls.

Smoke fills the room.

The smoke alarm beeps and shrieks, giving me a splitting headache.

I pull out my phone with trembling hands and dial 911 to report the fire.

Then I grab my purse and throw open the door to warn others.

Fed with oxygen, the fire roars with intensity and follows me.

I pound with my fists on the motel's second-story doors.

"Fire! Get out. Run for your lives."

I fly down the stairs and scream, knocking on doors until my knuckles are raw.

Going room to room, I hammer on doors and yell for people to exit.

Sirens wail in the distance, coming closer.

A fire truck chugs like a heavy beast down the dirt lane with a blaring siren.

The police arrive in a squad car, lights flashing.

My clothes are wet with sweat. I'm panting and out of breath. Clutching my churning stomach, I bend over and hang my head in shame.

Fire fighters jump off the rig, unreel hoses and spray

water on the fire. Dirty smoke billows into the dark night sky, obscuring stars.

Inhaling smoke, I break into a coughing fit. Cold night air seeps into my skin, and I rub my arms.

Firefighters battle the blaze with hoses and axes. I clear my throat. How will I ever make this right?

A police officer approaches me.

"I'm arresting you," she says, "for reckless burning. Come with me."

My teeth chatter as I walk to the squad car. There's no denying I did this. I've made the biggest mistake of my life.

1

Four months later, I'm sentenced in Okanagan County Superior Court for setting the fire. In Court, I pled guilty to reckless burning in the second degree, a gross misdemeanor, and I agreed to pay restitution of $100,000. The judge ordered me to make payments based on my income, so I'll pay $150 per month.

I was also fined three-thousand-dollars, which my mother paid. I'm not a freeloader. I just haven't saved money yet or found anything I want to do for work, which is how I ended up as a house cleaner employed by my mother.

When I stop by her brick rambler to see her, she says, "You look all worn out, with bags under your eyes. You spent four nights in jail, and you owe gobs of restitution money. Take a break for three days. I'll give you time off with pay. Hopefully after that, you won't leave the vacuum at a client's house or forget to empty their trash."

I sigh and take a strand of hair, twirling it around my index finger.

She slaps my hand. "And stop pulling your hair out by the roots."

I sit on my hands and groan, but she's right. I need to stop torturing myself for what I've done. In jail, I plucked out a chunk of hair, leaving a bald spot on my scalp. I guess it was a way of punishing myself.

My mom says, "That reporter keeps calling, and I'm tired of her pestering us. While you're away, I'll tell her you're out of town and unavailable."

I frown. "I don't want to talk to her. And why is her name Ned? I haven't figured that out."

My mom shrugs. "Maybe her birth name is Nedwina or something odd like that. Anyway, I'm responsible for what you did. I told you to light the candle and burn pages of your diary in the motel room. So, I'll pay the fine. But the rest is on you."

"Thanks, I'll pay you back when I'm done paying restitution to the motel owners."

She pats my back. "Hon, I think you'll be making those payments for the rest of your life. Interest really adds up."

Sitting at the round kitchen table, I rub my eyes with the palms of my hands. "I'm in debt and feeling a little overwhelmed. Will I ever climb out of the hole I dug?"

Mom sets a cup of jasmine tea in front of me. "Drink this, and you'll feel better. I added honey. Go away on a mini-vacation."

I look at her with wide eyes. "And how well did that work the last time?"

"Keep an open mind. Didn't you say you received an invitation to a resort up north near Millersville? Make a reservation for three nights. You can walk in the woods, write poetry, do whatever you need to do to start feeling better. Leave the guilt behind."

Tilting my head, I say, "Easy to say, but harder to do. It'll take more than a cup of tea and staying at a cabin to make me feel better."

"It could be worse."

I roll my eyes. "Exactly how?"

"Remember the woman who started a huge wildfire in Colorado? She spent years in prison, and her debt is over a million dollars and growing, with interest accumulating."

I nod. My situation isn't as bad as that. Still, I wish I'd never lit that match.

ON THE FREEWAY NORTH, I shake my head and scold myself as I navigate through gnarled Seattle traffic to Two Rivers Resort. What a fool I was to burn paper in a motel room. Or to light a candle. I should've used a fire pit outside. I'm lucky I didn't burn the place down. Instead, four units were damaged.

I pull up to the Two Rivers Resort office, located in a log cabin, and get out of the car. Thick evergreens in dense clusters crowd in, making the area dark. A dirt lane leads away from the office into the woods.

Inside, a man in his forties with wire-rimmed glasses looks up.

"I'm checking in for Cabin Eight."

He looks me over, and his eyes narrow. "Name?"

"Miranda Diggs."

"Driver's license?"

I hand it over. He studies it, holds it up and squints at me.

"Doesn't look like you. What happened to your hair?"

I blow out a breath. How mortifying. "Some of it fell out."

He frowns and fingers his thick eyebrows. "Well, you looked better before. I'd rather not rent to your type, but we need the money, so here's your key. No loud parties, whatever you do. And don't pet the coyotes."

When he laughs, his breath smells like cigars.

I grab the key and turn to go.

"Fire danger's high," he barks. "No fires. No campfires in the firepits."

I nod. Little does he know I'm responsible for a motel fire in the mountains. Do I know what a mistake that was? Yes, I regret it with every step I take and every swallow I make. Every breath I exhale is tainted with guilt. What's worse is how that reporter Ned keeps calling and asking to interview me. I just want to forget the whole episode and move on.

In Cabin Eight, I store my bag in the one-room cabin with a kitchenette, a round dining table and two double beds. When I open the closet there's one red mitten and a child's red tricycle. That's strange.

You'd think they'd clean up better before new guests check in. But not everyone is as professional as Diggs Cleaning. I take pride in my work and leave each place in better shape than when I arrived. Well, of course, that was before. I've become absent-minded, as my mother said. I left my vacuum at the Doughertys' two weeks ago and went home. The next day, I had to go back and retrieve it before going to the Gassers' house, which made me late for my appointments the rest of the day.

I lock the cabin and set out on foot to explore the grounds. Pinecones litter cabin roofs. Potholes in the dirt road are filled with water from the recent rain. The soles of my shoes crunch on pine needles underfoot.

Ahead, a sign points to a river trail. I turn and make my way down a hill. A canopy of tree branches blocks sunlight coming through the clouds, allowing intermittent light. A woman in her mid-thirties pushes a stroller up the slope. She stops, breathing hard and gripping the handles. I smile at her and continue on.

Going down and taking a tight switchback, I marvel at how she pushed the baby buggy up this rough dirt trail. My mind drifts. I have no idea if I want kids or to get married one day, maybe not in that order. I skid on pebbles on the path and brace for a fall, knees locking, but my feet fly out from under me. I land with a thud on my butt.

Rubbing my back, I get up and walk down to the river. The sound of rushing water might soothe some people, but for me it has the exact opposite effect. My hands clench into fists. Hairs on my arms stand on end. My eyes search out a rocky pool on the other side of the channel, where danger lurks. What if someone fell in? What would I do? Would I rescue them this time?

"Enough," I say. "Time to make peace. There's no going back."

I turn and hike up the trail, my thigh muscles complaining. The sun breaks through the clouds, warming my skin. I tromp back to the cabin and unlock the door.

It's time to follow my mother's new advice. She's an endless source of ideas for how I should shape and improve my life. I figure why not. I might as well give it a try.

But first, I brew a pot of coffee. A muddy brown liquid burbles on the stovetop in a dented metal percolator. I pull out my journal, which was the source of my recent troubles. I have two issues to contend with: haunting memories from summer camp and the fire at the mountain motel. I'm lugging around a backpack of rocky regrets.

The smell of burning coffee makes me jump up and turn off the stove. I pour steaming black coffee into a chunky, cream-colored ceramic mug and plunk down in a wobbly wooden chair. Maybe this time I'll get it right, and nothing terrible will happen.

2

A few minutes later, I'm tapping my pen on the table, gazing out the window. The resort is off a dirt road, and ten miles or more from the nearest town of Millersville. Tall evergreen trees and hills hem in ten cabins. Calling it isolated is an understatement. But the name *resort* really shouldn't be used to describe the place. It's a bunch of log cabins left over from a rundown camp, long forgotten and little used. I don't know why my mother picked this spot for me to recover from the trauma of starting a roaring fire.

Fooling around and not feeling like writing my thoughts down, I pick up my phone. Two weak bars of cell service connect me to the outside world. But it doesn't matter because I'm here to focus on my feelings and come to terms with what I've done.

When my phone rings, it's my mom, and I answer.

Apparently two bars of cell reception are enough for her to get through and ask probing questions.

"Hey, Mom."

"How's the resort? Is it as nice as the photos on the website made it look like?"

"It's in the middle of nowhere." I pull back the brown plaid curtains and look out at a dark forest. "And not many people around. It's almost deserted."

"You're not there to mix and mingle. Focus on you. That's what you're there for. Oh, the reporter called about the fire again. She really wants to interview you."

"I wish she'd stop hounding us."

Silence. I stare at the phone. No bars of cell service.

In case she can hear me, I say, "I'll see you in a few days. Love you."

I hang up and slide the phone into my pocket. The reporter wants to hear my side of the story. Why did I burn pages from my diary? What was it like when the curtains caught on fire? Could I have called for help earlier than I did?

Everyone I've seen in the last four months asks the same question. They stare at my missing patch of hair, which I've combed over without much success. Then they say, "Why did you do it?" Even that nice Mrs. Coleman with the huge home in the Highlands interrogated me. I shake my head now, knowing I deserve it. But the public scrutiny and pressure is getting to me.

I'm pacing the floor and restless, so I set out for a walk

in a different direction. Maybe that will clear my head. Down a dirt lane, a sign points to a Disc Golf Course.

Curious, I head in that direction and go into the woods, striding on a dirt path.

Three women in their early thirties carry small backpacks loaded with discs. Some are green, some are red, and one is gold with a sharp edge.

A woman with long brown hair pulled back in a ponytail raises her arm and throws a disc like a baseball player. With a clang, it hits the metal chains at the goalpost. It looks like she's talented at this sport.

I continue ahead, seeking solitude while I figure out what to say to Ned, the reporter. My foolishness caused the fire at the Riverdale Lodge. I never imagined there was danger when I lit the match. Fortunately, no one died, but rooms were damaged in the blaze. Of course, that's what I thought at camp. I had no idea when we stepped into the river that my friend would get carried away by the current.

"Join us," the pony-tailed pro-style playing woman says.

"Thanks, but I'll pass," I say. "Just out for a walk to clear my head."

A woman with short hair and a knit cap says, "It's fun."

"Maybe another time."

My phone buzzes, and I pull it out.

Ned, the reporter, texted. "Spoke with your mother. Need more background. Call me."

I'm about to turn it off to shut out the outside world

when a text comes through with a ding. It's from Ned again. "If you don't call me, I'll contact Natasha and Clarice to round out the story."

I groan. They're not only my best friends, but they're the biggest gossips. I've hardly seen them since the motel fiasco and have been keeping to myself. But I'm sure if the reporter interviews those two, my private life will be spread all over the news for strangers to read while eating breakfast. I'll be ripped open by trolls on social media.

I text Ned. "I'll be back in Seattle in three days. Will be in a no cell service area until then."

Turning off the phone, I stride ahead. About twenty yards off the path is a derelict weather-beaten barn with a No Trespassing sign. The building sits in a field and looks like it hadn't been used in years. For some reason, I'm drawn to it. I can't resist going over and seeing if I can open the door.

The door slides open with a smooth glide, as if someone recently used it.

Inside the barn, the air is still. Dust motes float in the air. Faint filtered light comes through a dirty window.

I step inside, wanting to be distracted from my woes and worries. As dust rises, I sneeze. The place smells of mold and mildew.

Writing on the wall catches my eye, so I go over to read it.

"Don't come here. This is Mr. Nobody's Place."

The handwriting is shaky, as if the person who wrote

it was agitated. The words are written in charcoal and slightly streaked, but I can still make out what it says. As a cold chill creeps up my spine, I rub my arms.

Coming here was a mistake. I should have stayed home and dealt with my problems head on. Instead, I've cornered myself with only my thoughts as company.

I'd imagined peace and comfort at Cabin Eight. In my mind, I'd be tucked among the trees and arrive at hard truths and realizations I could share with the world about my part in the fire.

My pulse quickens. If Ned the reporter probes into my past, she'll find out about the accident when I was young. I don't want that to happen. I must stop her at any cost.

I'm about to leave the barn when footsteps approach outside.

"She went in there?" a woman says.

A second female says, "Yep, marched right in, ignored the signs."

"We'll teach her not to mess with other people's property."

The barn door slides shut. A flurry of dust makes me cough. The sound of a metal clasp snicks shut.

"Hey." I run to the door and pull on it.

It doesn't open. My hands are sweaty. I pound on the wood. The door is locked from the outside.

I throw my shoulder into it, but the door won't budge.

"Let me out. You can't trap me like this. Don't lock me in."

The women laugh.

"She'll learn."

"The hard way, like the others did."

Footsteps move away. Sticks underfoot crackle and snap.

Breaking into a sweat, I scream. "Let me out."

A woman chuckles. "See if you can find your way out. No one has yet."

The other says, "She won't escape. She likes to keep to herself. Too stuck up to hang out with us."

Panting hard, I pound on the window as they walk away.

"Don't leave me. Come back."

3

The women leave, fading into the forest. I yell for help until my throat is raw. Metal bars mounted over the windows trap me inside. I can't wiggle out through the four-inch gaps.

A still silence grows around me in the stuffy old barn. I pull out my cell phone to dial 911, but I don't have cell reception here. I try texting my mother to call the police, but when I press send, nothing happens.

I frown. I'm deep in the woods. The resort office is a mile back off a two-lane road. No one will hear my cries for help.

My stomach growls, but's the least of my worries. I gaze out through the smudged glass. A turkey buzzard circles in search of a carcass, which is what I'll be if I don't hurry up and find a way out.

Inhaling a deep breath, I break into a coughing fit.

Dust motes swirl. I wish I hadn't wandered into the barn, going past warning signs. Once again, I let my curiosity steer me into trouble.

Pacing the floor, I pick up a rusted pitchfork and push strands of hay aside. A round metal ring is screwed into a square of wood cut into the floor. Is it a way out? If so, where does it go? Would I be better off waiting for the women to come back and release me than trying to escape this way? From the sound of their banter, it didn't sound like they planned to return.

Who were those women and why did they lock me inside? Was it part of a strange, sadistic game?

I scan the space for past wanderers' remains and shriek.

Yellow eyes blink in a dim corner.

A cat hisses, arching its back.

"You're stuck in here too? We'll get out if I have to ram the door down."

Releasing a shaky breath, I bend and touch the cold metal ring. I must gather the courage to open it. Grasping the metal ring, I tug, straining my shoulders.

A damp smell comes out from open hole.

A hint of foul decay lingers in the air.

The cat purrs and rubs against my legs.

"Let's see what's down there."

Using my phone as a flashlight, I peer down. My hands are cold and damp. A narrow dirt tunnel beckons, but I didn't want to climb down into it. I might get stuck. It could lead nowhere with no place to turn around.

My heart thuds as I glance around the barn, looking for other ways out. Several feet away is a canvas-covered contraption. I march over and pull off the tarp.

A John Deere green riding lawn mower sits as if ready to start up and mow the grass. The key is in the ignition. I smile. Excellent. This escape method is far better than crawling through a cobwebbed tunnel.

But I step back and tap my lips. The cat meows. I didn't see a lawn to mow on the resort grounds. We're in the middle of a forest.

A metal bucket for digging is attached to the front. Something strikes me as suspicious.

I climb on the seat to drive it through the barn doors, knocking them down. It'll be a grand exit and an up yours to the women who locked me in.

But when I turn the key, the engine doesn't cough, whimper, or whine.

The battery is dead.

Searching in fading light, I can't find a power outlet or electrical cord to charge the battery. But a red can of gasoline is on the floor against a wall. Lifting it, I nod. It's half full. If I don't find another way out, I'll set a fire by the doors to blow them open.

I shake my head. That's an erroneous idea that tops them all. Smoke inhalation would kill me before the doors burned down.

One of my downfalls is I'm fascinated with fire. I keep a Bic lighter in my jeans pocket and a pack of matches in my purse. Sure, I'd blow the doors wide open eventually, but the cat and I would perish in the process.

I return to the dark pit in the floor. It reminds me of something I've seen in nightmares. The gaping hole is dark and dusty. Because it looks like it's been used in the past, it could lead to freedom, or I could break my neck.

My hands tremble as I aim the phone's flashlight beam.

I couldn't make out much of what's down below, just brown dirt and a tight passageway.

I crane my neck and lean forward. The cat walks between my feet, wrapping around my ankles. As I push her away from the opening, I pitch forward and fall, tumbling down.

I claw the dirt with my fingernails, trying to get a grip and stop my descent. I brace my legs but find no foothold. Down I go, down into the dark.

With a thud, I land and howl with pain. My ankles and knees ache. The air is still. Where am I?

When I stand up, I grope around on the dirt floor. I dropped my phone. I touch something furry and yelp. The cat yowls.

My heart races. The walls close in on me. I can't breathe.

I pick up the cat so it wouldn't be scared, and the creature meows.

"There, there," I say, petting soft fur.

As the cat purrs, my pulse slows.

I'm not sure where I am or who might hear me, so I whisper, "We'll get out of here. I hope. Eventually."

My elbow aches and is wet with blood. My knees felt like I've done a hundred squats. I clear my parched throat and move on, hunching over so I don't hit my head.

As I shuffle forward, a dim light beckons ahead.

The cat jumps out of my arms and lands with a thud.

Taking hesitant steps, I pat the narrow passage's cool, damp earthen walls.

When the cat steps in front of me, I stumble and suck in a breath of stagnant air.

"Stay behind. Be a good cat and go find my phone."

I'm definitely losing it from being confined. I'm talking to a cat.

I detect a faint breeze. Maybe there is a reason to hope, and I'm approaching an exit. A smell of burning sage or marijuana lingers, and I cough. A headache throbs.

Shuffling along, I stumble into a brightly lit underground cave.

A woman with a wrinkled face and long gray braids sits beside a circle of stones, meditating. Her index fingers and thumbs touch, resting in her lap.

"Who are you?" I say. "And where am I?"

She opens her eyes. "Did you bring the cat?"

"Yes, I did. Does it matter?"

She arches her eyebrows. "You'd be surprised how few

people bring Brutus with them."

She stands and stretches, shifting from side to side and reaching out with long-fingered hands. "Join me for tea. Make yourself at home. We'll talk and then you and Brutus will leave."

My head spins in the surreal setting. "Brutus?"

"The cat. Of course. Haven't you been paying attention?"

I shrug. Nothing is making sense. I'm confused.

"Do you know why those women locked me in the barn?"

"Oh, honey, wake up. You've been telling yourself nonsense. You're not innocent, you know. You caused the disaster."

My eyes open wide.

"I don't understand."

"Think about it. Your whole approach to life is wrong. Here we are in an underground room, and you still don't get it?"

I cock my head.

"No, I don't."

She pats the space next to her on the hard-packed dirt floor.

"Come and sit beside me. We'll talk. You'll learn."

As I settle beside her, I'm quaking inside.

I try to summon a hint of a smile.

"I'm not sure why I'm here, or why the cat is so important."

4

The woman flicks back her long, gray braids. She straightens the folds of her loose ankle-length dress. She sighs. "Now that you're here, let's begin."

I raise my eyebrows, not sure what I'm getting into. The cat stalks over to a dark corner. This woman may be part of a plot to kidnap me or a wise person who somehow knows my innermost secrets.

Her eyes close. "You take and take, with no regrets."

"Pardon me? What're you talking about?"

"You started a fire and could've killed people. What were you thinking, foolishly lighting a candle in your motel room? Are you aware of the damage you caused?"

I gasp at how much she knows. But it has been on the news. Sniffling, I rub my nose. Until now, I've done what feels right and haven't given a thought to others.

"I pled guilty in court, and I'm paying restitution. It's no business of yours."

She swirls a stick in the air, making a figure eight over our heads.

"You need to tell the owners of the motel you're sorry. Have you done that yet?"

My jaw clamps shut. Her voice is gentle and kind. This whole cave meeting with a stranger is weird, and so is the part about the cat. I can't wrap my head around it. I'm not sure who she is or what I'm doing here.

She stares at me with clear blue eyes, as if waiting for a reply.

"I want to go home. How do I get out of here? I'll pack my things, and some other lucky soul can have Cabin Eight."

"There's no way out. We research and screen our guests before they arrive to be sure their pasts are without blemishes. But we made an exception for you, this one time."

I swallow hard.

"I don't want to be the exception. If I'd known it'd be like this, I never would've come. We're at a dead end of hell with no turn around."

"Sassy, aren't you? Throwing words around like spears. I bet your mother is ashamed of you, deep down."

I clap a hand to my heart. This stranger knows how to wound me in my deepest depths. How does she know so much about me? I cross my fingers and hope it's a ruse or a devious psychological test designed to test one's mental stability and how they adapt. If that's the case, I'm failing fast.

"My mother and I are very close. I'm sure she doesn't think anything like that."

She crosses her arms. "If that's true, why did she speak with a reporter today and divulge personal details you don't want made public?"

I stare at her. "What do you mean?"

She cackles. "Didn't you hear? Before you barged into the barn, she talked with the reporter Ned. She told her all about the fire in Lazama. How you went across the mountains to have a ritual. You lit a candle and burned pages from your diary. Detectives found partial pages in the debris. It was incriminating, wasn't it? You've never spoken to the press about that."

A chill runs up my spine.

"It's private. No one's supposed to know that."

"But we do." She stands, dusting off her skirt. "Shall we go?"

Dread sweeps over me as I get up.

Looking around the cave, I say, "Go where? I don't see a way out."

She takes a headlamp from a niche in the wall and straps it on her head.

"Take the other one."

Wrapping the nylon band around, I adjust the light.

She claps her hands, and a rope ladder drops down from the ceiling.

Grabbing it and stopping it from swaying, she puts her right foot on it.

"Follow me. But whatever you do, don't look down."

Up she goes, climbing the rope rungs. My chest tightens. I'd counted on having a short break at Two Rivers Resort, not a strange endurance test. Where was the cat, anyway? It couldn't climb a rope, could it?

Taking the rough hemp in my hands, I remember my phone and let the ladder go.

"I've got to go back and get my phone."

She pauses mid-step, not looking down, "If you do, that's the last you'll see of me. You'll lose hope of attaining a meaningful life. Kiss it goodbye."

"I can find it with this light. I need it, to call out and for emergencies."

"How's that worked for you so far here? Did the phone help you in the barn?"

I shrug. "It didn't help. But I can't afford a new one. I'm going back for it."

"Like I said, it's your pick. Your phone or your life. Get the phone and find your way back to the barn. Or go up this way and find out what's next. Your choice."

My hands tremble. I miss my phone. I almost feel my fingers around it. It was so familiar and part of me. I can't leave it in the tunnel. How will I call or text anyone?

"Last chance. Come up or stay behind. The opening will close soon."

I take a shallow breath, wipe my moist hands on my pants and step on the rope ladder's bottom rung. This is crazy, but I'm going along with it. I have no idea what's behind me in the dark, but she seems like someone I could trust. She's so sure of herself. I could use more of that.

"Hold on. Wait for me. I don't know where I'm going."

She laughs. "That's the first sensible thing you've said all day."

My head snaps up as I climb. She's wearing yoga pants under her skirt.

"How do you know all that you said?"

"Honey, we know everything. This isn't your normal type resort."

My jaw drops open, and my mind whirls with ideas.

"Do you have a surveillance camera in my cabin?"

"Yep."

"And along the trail?"

"Uh huh. Now you're cluing in."

"How about in the barn?"

"Of course, it's for our guests' protection. And you're one of the lucky ones."

I groan and make the mistake of looking down. A wave of dizziness slams into me. We're twenty or more feet up and climbing.

"I wouldn't say I'm lucky at all. It's almost like I'm

marked with a dark cloud. Everywhere I go, something bad happens."

"You can change that, you know."

"Right," I say, rolling my eyes. "With positive visualization and exercise? I know all about that. Didn't work for me. Mark me off as a loss, one of those who didn't quite get a grip on life's ladder of success."

She doesn't say anything, but I can hear her breathing.

My thighs scream from the ascent. My palms sting from gripping the spiky rope.

"How much farther?"

"Now you're sounding like a five-year-old. Not far yet. Just a little bit more."

"What's at the top? Or who?"

"You'll see. Stop worrying and letting your curiosity drive you. Just relax and trust me."

I snort. "Trust you? I don't even know who you are or why I'm here."

"You had enough information to follow me, didn't you? You've learned we know all about you, about things you thought you'd kept hidden. And we haven't even begun to talk about what happened in the river that day."

My throat closes tight, and I clamp my lips shut. Nothing good will come from pressing her for details. I don't want to talk about the disaster at the river. Best if we leave that subject buried, except I haven't managed to put it in the past and forget it.

5

Climbing the rope ladder, my shoulders ache from when I scraped the skin, tumbling down the tunnel. My elbow twinges with pain. My knees complain. Thick rope digs into my palms and cuts my fingertips.

"Here we are," she says, pointing to a platform to our right.

Her movements are agile. The fabric of her long skirt whispers as she hops. If that were me, I'd trip and fall head first down to the dirt floor, breaking my neck.

My stomach turns over.

"I don't think I can jump over where you are. It looks far. I might fall."

"Come on now, I did it. You just watched me. I'm at least twice your age. If I can jump, you can."

My breath is shallow.

"I didn't sign up for this. I just want to hang out for a few days at a cabin. I thought being off the grid might clear my head."

"And yet since you've been here, you've done nothing but check your phone and text and call people. No wonder you can't concentrate. It's better you left it behind."

The weight of my situation sits on me like a sumo wrestler. I don't want to jump, but I must to move on and get out of here. My knees shake, standing on a rung of the rope ladder. I want my phone. I need my phone. I want to call my mother and find out if this woman told the truth about her blabbing to a reporter.

I blow out a breath. My grip on the rope weakens. My fingers ache.

A tear trickles down my cheek. What have I gotten myself into?

"Don't panic now," she says. "You can do this. Picture yourself taking the giant step and easily moving to the platform."

In a tight voice, I say, "Is there an elevator option?"

"No, I'm sorry there isn't. This way is not for sissies or cowards. You're tough, and you can do it."

I eye the platform. It isn't far, like she says, just a foot or so.

The rope ladder suddenly swings from side to side.

I hold on and yelp.

I look down.

A man with a bushy brown beard down below shakes the ladder back and forth.

"Remember what I said?" the woman says to me. "Look up. Don't look down."

She calls, "Lane, stop that. She's about to jump. Then you can get on with your chores."

My brows furrow, pondering what kind of chores Lane might have in a cave. I stare at the platform where the wise woman stands. I can do it. I must jump.

"Here's a secret," she says. "Grab the chain that's coming from the ceiling."

The pit of my stomach drops. I'm not an acrobat.

Drawing a deep breath, I tense my muscles.

Leaping off the ladder, I grab a metal chain and swing onto the platform.

I land and clutch a support with both hands.

Panting hard, my muscles tremble as adrenaline surges through my body.

"I never want to do that again."

She says, "Then I won't tell you what's ahead."

She offers a warm, dry hand, and I take it to steady myself.

Then I dust myself off.

"Now what?"

"Why don't you tell me?"

Tilting my head, I say, "How would I know?"

"I don't. The game changes each time. Otherwise, it's not as much fun."

"I wouldn't call this fun, more like a game of holding me hostage and mind control."

She pats my back as if reassuring me.

She bellows, hands around her mouth, "Malice, open the side door."

Silence follows.

I bite my lower lip. What am I doing here? This is ridiculous. From now on, if I get out alive, I'll stay in the city. No more life-changing solo retreats for me that turn bad.

"Malice? Did you hear me?"

Feet shuffle.

We're teetering on a narrow platform with a long way to fall.

I clench my teeth and wait to see what will happen.

Nothing changes.

The woman nudges me. "Say something. See if you can open the door."

I think for a beat and say in a loud, clear voice, "Do you have the cat?"

A door in the wall behind us slides open.

"Greetings," a thin man in his forties says. He's dressed in a tuxedo, and his black hair is slicked back. "You uttered the secret code. Right this way."

I step through the doorway. It's warm and dry away from the cave. Heat shimmers off earthen walls. My armpits are damp with sweat. I take off my jeans jacket and carry it.

Following the man in the tuxedo, I sniff the air and smell sage.

"Where are you taking me?"

He stops and turns around.

"Turn off your headlamp," he says, "you're blinding me."

I turn the light off but leave it in place because I might need it later.

He flips a switch on the wall, and soft lights illuminate a path ahead.

As we walk, the rumblings of working machinery grow loud.

A door slams.

Crumbling dirt falls from the ceiling into my eyes.

I cough and rub earth from my eyes. Leaning over, I brush dirt from my hair.

I need his help to get to Cabin Eight. From there, I'll hop in my car and race home, never to return to the deep, dark forest. I'll never wander into an old barn again or ignore No Trespassing signs. If I manage to get home, I'll be a good person. I'll hug my mother every day and tell her I love her and appreciate all she's done for me. I'll make a fresh start.

"Would you please tell me what's going on?" I say. "Can you help us?"

When I turn around to confirm with the wise woman in the long dress, she's not there. I didn't see any doors. She must've stayed on the platform.

In her place is a short, hairy man with large feet. He comes up to my shoulders, and his grin is as wide as Lake Washington.

"Howdy," he says. "I'm bringing up the rear. In case you try to turn around, I want you to know there's no backtracking. Webbings have a policy of only going forward. We never go back." He shakes a finger. "In special cases, we may approve a circle route, but only in the case of a guaranteed return journey."

I blink. The rules in this earth mound aren't like those I know. I must find my way out. I wonder aloud, "Is anything guaranteed?"

Mr. Tuxedo clears his throat. "Howdy would like to think so. Let's keep going, or we'll be late."

"Late for what?"

The sound of metal gears grinding is louder than my voice.

We pass an open door, and I glance inside.

Steam hisses from a pipe, shooting up and out a smokestack in the ceiling.

"What's going on in there?"

Mr. Tuxedo says, "We're preparing for the coming complete power grid failure. There'll be a total loss of electricity, nuclear power, and the power grid. We'll be ready. We're working on a solution while others are ignoring the problem hovering on the horizon."

I say, "Between being trapped in the barn and this

kind of talk, you're freaking me out. I just came to the resort for a short vacation."

Mr. Tuxedo raises his eyebrows and stares. "And to burn more pages during a burn ban? We know who you are. You can't hide from us. You need counseling for your hunger for fire and your propensity for breaking rules. You blindly follow your curiosity wherever it leads, like into an old barn."

I nod. "You have a point."

"Give her a break," Howdy says. "She's only here for a few days. You can't expect her to become a convert."

Cocking my head, I say, "Is this some sort of cult? If so, I want out right now. Let me run to my car, and you'll never see me again."

"We can't let you do that. Ms. Spectrum said you had special skills. No one else can solve the X factor problem."

I hold up my hands. "I'm a nobody. I don't possess special skills. There must be a misunderstanding."

On our right, double doors open to a cafeteria. Hundreds of people sit at tables, talking and eating what must be lunch or dinner. I don't know what time it is without my phone. My stomach growls. The smell of beef chili with beans, my favorite dish, wafts by.

Howdy gestures inside. "That's right. We know your favorite dish, and today, all the workers are eating it."

Weaving our way through the vast room, we made our way to the back of the food line. Ten people step aside as one.

"Right this way, to the front of the line," Mr. Tuxedo says.

"I don't want to go first," I say, "I'll take a tray and wait for my turn."

Howdy looks deep into my eyes. "Did you do that when you were twelve at summer camp?"

I scuff a foot. Somehow, these people know all my secrets.

"No, I didn't. I'll admit it, I barged ahead for breakfast the first day. No one stopped me, so I was always first in line. Now I know that was rude, and I shouldn't have done it."

Mr. Tuxedo points to the waiting people, who as one moved back in line to be served food ahead of us. "Sounds like it's a lesson learned then, eh?"

"I guess."

Howdy says, "You're not taking your rehabilitation seriously, are you?"

"I didn't sign up for that. I just came here to collect my thoughts."

Mr. Tuxedo says, "And perhaps to start another fire? What motel owner in their right mind would allow you to rent a cabin for even one night?" He sets a cafeteria tray down and waves his arms. "You're like, who cares if the world burns. If I'm fine, that's all that matters. Is that right?"

Shame sweeps over me, and my face heats. For the last

few hours, I'd forgotten I started the motel fire in the mountains. My secret is out.

"Chili, please," Tuxedo says to a cafeteria worker. He's in front of me in line. She serves him.

The whine of machinery comes through the walls.

"A bowl of chili, please," I say. "With cheese and crackers on top."

"I'm sorry," the middle-aged woman with her hair tied back says. "We just sold the last of it. You'll have to pick something else."

"What else do you have?"

She points to a white board. "All items are listed over there."

Chili is crossed out. Only eggplant remains. I'd rather chew on a log than eat that. But I'm hungry, and I want to stay in my hosts' good graces in order to find my way out.

"I'll have the eggplant."

Just then, a woman climbs up on a ladder and crosses out that option.

"Sorry, no more of that left."

"What do you have, if everything's gone?"

"Oatmeal, leftover from yesterday's breakfast."

My stomach sours. Gruel sounds awful. "Thanks, I'll take a bowl."

"Only enough for a cup." She slams her plexiglass window shut in my face.

I look around for my companions, but Tuxedo and

Howdy are gone. Workers file out of the cafeteria, leaving me alone. "Where do I get the food?"

Behind her plexiglass shield, she points to the far end of the room, where an old man sits at a cash register. He looks as alone as I feel. Walking the long, linoleum-tiled way, I wonder if I'd ever get out of here and make my way home.

6

"What'd you order?" the old man says.

"Oatmeal," I say.

He glances at the board. "We're not offering that today."

"I know, but you were out of everything else. I don't like oatmeal, but I'm hungry."

He eyes me. "Are you a whiner? It sounds like you are. If so, I have the right to refuse service."

He closes the cash register till and walks away.

"Please, I'm hungry," I say in a loud voice that echoes in the empty room. I'm the only one here. All the other customers left. "Have a heart."

He pivots in place and comes back to confront me, pointing at me.

"You have the nerve to ask me to have a heart? What about the little girl who fell into the water and died at summer camp? All because of you and your recklessness."

Tears stream down my cheeks.

"Please, don't bring that up. I'm trying to forget what happened."

He plucks at a wild white eyebrow hair.

"But you couldn't, could you? Because you were partly responsible."

Nodding, I say, "I'm responsible for that girl's death, and I don't care who knows it. I shouldn't have distracted her when she was wading in the river by the rapids. The current pulled her away."

Breaking down in tears, I cover my face with my hands. My shoulders shudder. I'd wanted to forget how I caused Fiona's death, but events like this keep bringing it back.

The cash register till opens with a ding.

He pulls out a golden key and hands it to me.

"This is your reward for your honesty. Don't blame yourself. It could've happened to anyone."

Wiping my eyes on my sleeve, I sniffle and take the heavy key.

"What does this go to?"

He shrugs. "Heck if I know."

"And what about the food? The oatmeal I ordered?"

He glances over his shoulder to the clattering kitchen. "Sorry, the kitchen is closed. Come back for the next meal, if you can find us. Our location is always moving."

On a table is a packet of crackers in a clear plastic wrapper. I grab it and stuff it into my pocket to eat when I'm out of sight of the Cash Register Man.

"Don't eat those," he calls as I leave the room. "They'll make you sick. You'll grow so tall you won't fit through windows or doors. You won't be able to get to Cabin Eight or ever get home."

With a groan, I toss the crackers in a trash can.

I'm hungry and alone, wandering in a huge industrial underground complex. I have no one to depend on but myself. All I have is a gold metal key, and I have no idea what it unlocks.

Hurrying down the hall, my stomach rumbles. I glance around. People on this side of the complex are wearing blue uniforms, like scrubs nurses and doctors wear under white coats.

"You, there," a woman's deep voice calls. "Stop. Don't proceed."

She approaches and stands close, staring at my pupils.

"I see you didn't eat the crackers. Good. That would have been a major problem, to remove you from the premises if you were ten times as big as you are now."

I hold out the key. "Do you know where this goes? And might you have some food to eat? A snack of some sort?"

I dig in my pocket for something to trade and pull out a big red paper clip.

"This is all I have to pay with."

She jumps back and shields her eyes.

"Put that away right now. It could mess with the signals we rely on for our circuitry. You could single-handedly bring our alternate industrial complex to its knees. After all our work and so many years building this community with willing volunteers, we can't take a chance of you destroying it."

I hold it up. "But I just want some pretzels or graham crackers or chocolate. Or cheese?"

She wrinkles her nose. "Cheese? You still eat that? We stopped eating dairy here two years ago. What a naïve part of the world you come from."

She grabs my wrist and pulls me down the hall.

"Right this way to the destroyer-matic. We put all our dangerous recyclable metal in the Otronic machine. I'll show you. But whatever you do," she says, taking me into a white stark, chilly room, "Don't."

"Look down?"

She shakes her head. "Don't let your jacket sleeve get caught in the rollers or it'll pull you in. That's not how you want to go. Better to save your end for something flashy, like paddling a canoe over a waterfall. Or," she eyes me, "getting caught in rapids in a swift-moving river."

I tilt my head. "Nice try, but I'm not as sensitive as that. The old man at the cash register helped me work through it."

She arches a brow. "He did, did he? I thought I was supposed to play that part."

Coming to a whirring machine, she says, "Toss the

paperclip in, and let's go do something else besides saving the world."

Holding it in my hand, I realize the forbidden paper clip might give me a way out. It could be a bargaining chip if it came to a tough situation. I could threaten them with it.

When I pretend to toss it in and turn away, she says, "Nice try, missy, but that's not how we play. Throw it in, then we'll go find the door your key fits."

With a sigh, I insert the red paperclip into the moving metal teeth.

"There, that's done."

She watches as the machine chews it up, grinding away.

As a light flashes, an automated voice says: "Thank you for saving the Webby system, one paperclip at a time."

"Come on," she says, taking my elbow and guiding me down the hall. "Let's try a few doors to see what opens."

Going down the hall, I stick the key into several doors, but nothing unlocks.

Behind large rectangular windows in the hallway, scientists in white lab coats and safety goggles work with test tubes and petri dishes.

"What're they doing?"

She puts a finger to her lips. "Top secret project. Can't tell you, or I'll die."

After we've tried many interior doors, we come to a steel exit door.

I'm about to insert my gold key when she rushes me away.

"No time for that. You're not authorized to insert objects into the exterior exit doors. You haven't achieved the required status or level of mental peacefulness. In fact, I can tell right now, you're agitated and angry with me, aren't you?"

I screw up my face and put my hands on my hips.

"Of course, I'm angry and upset with you now. Who wouldn't be? You steer me away from going outdoors when all I want is to go home. Getting out of here makes sense to me. Don't you think so?"

She leans in and says in a confidential tone, "We can't allow fresh air to enter the premises. It's hermetically sealed. Only recycled, filtered air is allowed, or the machines will seize. Our workers will catch colds."

"But I came in from outside. You're letting me walk around."

"You didn't know it, but when you fell, we washed you with cleaning solution in the tunnel. It happened so fast you didn't realize it."

I shake my head. "I don't believe you. The cat was with me the whole time. No one would do that to a poor, unsuspecting creature like that."

She snaps her fingers. "You are caught in a lie. And you mentioned the cat. Where is he?"

"I don't know. Why?"

"The cat is the key to your getting out. You need to find her. Or all is lost."

Standing in the middle of the hall, I cross my arms.

"This sounds like a bunch of hooey to me. Everyone is making things up. I don't need a cat. I've got a key."

When I hold it up in the air, she grabs it and grins.

"You had it. Now, it's mine. Good luck getting it back."

She turns on her heels and marches off, moving fast, and uses the key to unlock an office. She goes inside, locks the door, and pulls down the blinds.

When I knock on the window glass, she pulls the blinds apart.

"Find another way out. We're busy in here."

7

Without the key, I'm lost, wandering the halls. No one looks my way.

Entering a laboratory with workstations, I stop and sniff the air, detecting vinegar and something else. Is that lime juice and tequila? A blender whirs, and I go over to inspect what a young goggle-wearing woman with short black hair is doing.

"Are you making margaritas?"

She puts a finger to her lips.

"Don't tell anyone. We're not supposed to eat or drink in the labs."

I glance around, searching for a clock to orient myself. I've lost track of time since sneaking into the barn. The walls are covered with charts of periodic tables and Far Side comics. A rectangular white board hung on the wall shows writing in blue marker: "Top priority IL-XB123 + IL-XZ456 bivalent. Test on human subjects Tuesday."

I gulp. "Testing on humans? Here? Are they volunteers, I hope?"

She pours margarita slush into five red plastic cups.

"Don't worry about it. We won't test it on you. Just on the others."

Raising my eyebrows, I scan the room for people who look like test subjects. "Who are the others? Where are they?"

"They're being brought in from the large barn on the edge of the property."

When I exhale audibly, she says, "Not the barn you were in."

She points to two monitors mounted on the wall showing surveillance footage of the world outside. Tall grass sways in a breeze. On one screen is the barn I was in. A second monitor shows another, bigger barn, where a group of frowning women stare through barred windows. They look ferocious. I wouldn't want to mess with them.

"We were watching you. I was hoping you'd find the trap door. Not everyone identifies that option or has the courage to go down the tunnel."

"The cat pushed me," I say. "But there are other ways out?"

She shrugs. "Sure, it's all part of the game to occupy us while we work on a cure for a world health disaster that's looming. We've been hired to work in shifts, sleeping in cots in side rooms, until we find the cure for the next onslaught of disease. It's going to be bad, and we're here to save the world. Of course, we're also making bank. Otherwise, we wouldn't have taken these assignments."

A headache throbs, and I rub my temples. Is this real? How could an underground laboratory with a secret crew of scientists working on a cure for a life-threatening illness hide from the rest of the world?

I need to find a phone or use a computer to send an email. I'll tell my mother to alert Ned, the reporter, to the covert operation. Ned pestered me and doesn't give up. She's called so often I know her phone number. She'd help me get out, and she'd be glad to blow their cover.

An image on the monitor catches my attention, and I stop thinking about myself. The women in the big barn are shaking their fists and shouting. Their faces are twisted in rage, and their mouths are snarling.

"What about them? Are they volunteers? Or were they lured here with false promises, like I was? What a ruse you pulled, sending an email and following up with a mailed invitation."

Making air quotes with my fingers, I say, "Enjoy a special soothing, healing solo retreat that comes at a dramatic discount. You've been selected for a stay at Two Rivers Resort. Cabin Eight is waiting for you. Come find renewal."

This whole experience is so weird, I let out a cackle.

How stupid was I to believe it was a valid offer and that I'd get anything out of it.

Just my luck that instead of knitting myself together at Cabin Eight, I'm coming apart and faced even more with my past. Underground, no less. I never should have wandered into the off-limits barn.

She pulls off her goggles, exposing dark brown eyes, and sets them on the counter.

Cupping her hands, she calls, "Party time. Come and get it. Drinks are ready. Bring the chips."

To me, she says, "I'm the lead scientist, so they follow my orders. The others will be here in a minute. They want to meet you and congratulate you on getting out of the barn. It's the first step. Not many get that far."

Frowning, I ponder how to get to the cabin, where I'll jump in my car and race home. I've got to get out of here. The underground facility is huge. I'm caught in a maze, pacing endless white hallways. I could grab her and hold her as hostage, using her retina or thumb print for the biometric scan to open doors.

"So, I'm not the first to get locked in that barn?"

She cocks her head, looking at me as if I'm crazy.

"Of course not."

"What happened to the others?"

She waves a hand. "No need to think about them. We have protocols and procedures to deal with failures."

I swallow hard, wondering what happened to those people. My mind churns with possibilities.

"Were they incinerated or buried alive or flown out and dropped in a remote valley, where they had to survive on local flora and fauna? Or are they drugged and forced to serve on an assembly line for whatever drug you're making?"

"Hah," she laughs with a twinkle in her eyes. "Now you're catching on. We have many possibilities open to us, and I'm not allowed to disclose trade secrets."

"I'm not a failure, so what does that make me?"

Ms. Goggles runs her fingers through her hair. "You're a test subject under observation. You don't have long in our lab. We programmed a brief rest period for you, and then you need to move on."

"I want to get back to the cabin. I need to go home. How do I get out of here?"

"You'll have to solve that problem on your own. We aren't allowed to help you."

My hands turn cold. "Let me borrow your phone. I'd like to call my mother."

She shakes her head. "Nice that you care so much about her, but sorry, I can't. We were instructed not to assist you. Especially if you asked for a phone."

"My mom will be worried about me," I say. "I promised to call and check in, let her know how my solo retreat is going. It won't take long. Please, let me use your phone."

She throws up her hands. Her fingers are long with manicured fingernails painted in blood red polish.

"You're out of luck. They take our phones when we come into work and put them in lock boxes. They're obsessed with preventing corporate espionage. And it helps ensure we're working, not messing around playing games on our phones or texting."

Blowing out a breath, I wonder how far it is to the two-lane road running past the resort. Traffic was light when I arrived. Only the occasional semi-truck and car went past. I'll be better off running to my car and driving away than hitchhiking on a quiet street where they might catch me and bring me back.

I say, "Sounds like security is tight."

She nods. "Extremely tight. Most doors have retinal scans. They're upgrading the system. Not all exit doors are secured like that."

I shiver, and goosebumps prick my flesh. I'm trapped and caught in a game I don't want to play. I'll have to try all the exit doors until I break through one without the retinal scan security.

A thought occurs to me. This might be how the motel owners felt when I burned down my room and part of the second floor. They lacked enough insurance coverage and couldn't rebuild. Their plans for the future were skunked, all because of my actions that fateful night.

Like coming here, I went to the motel to have a reckoning with myself. I figured it was time to turn toward the future and stop beating myself up about the past.

The pages were covered with pink and purple gel pen

cramped handwriting. I couldn't bear to revisit the haunted, naked ramblings of myself as a twelve-year-old girl. My worst days vanished in smoke. I wouldn't be able to revisit and read my defeated musings about the death at summer camp again. Finally, I could leave my self-blame behind.

That night, I shivered in the shadows near the motel owners, who wept as they watched their business burn. The middle-aged couple told me they'd bought the motel a few months ago. They'd moved from the city to leave urban crime behind.

In a single day, I'd ruined their rustic, rural dreams of a happy new life.

That night I knew I'd never be able to leave my dark past behind.

Later, a persistent reporter in Seattle informed me the motel owners didn't have enough insurance coverage to rebuild. They closed their business. Instead of heralding a new beginning for myself, I'd ruined two people's lives.

The worst part is, I never apologized to the owners except for offering a hurried remorseful comment the night of the fire. They'd looked so stunned, standing there with ashen faces, that I didn't want to bother them. Grimacing now with guilt, I make a vow. If I get out of here, the first thing I'll do is say I'm sorry. The former owners need to hear that, and I need to cough up that furball.

Reminded of the cat, I glance around. The laboratory

is clean and stark. No signs of a feline in sight. On the monitor, women in the large barn are pointing at the camera and shaking their fists. The volume is turned down, so I can't hear what they're saying.

It gives me the creeps, and a chill runs up my spine.

What kind of place is this?

Did my past mistakes drag me into this frightening mess?

8

Ms. Goggles glances at the group of about ten women in the large barn. She pulls out a notebook and writes a few lines before closing it and tucking it in a drawer.

"Things are building to a head in the big barn," she says. "That's not good for our test subjects. Cortisol levels in their blood will be elevated."

I tilt my head. "Why is that?"

"Cortisol is a stress hormone. It surges in flight or fight situations, when your blood pressure and heart rate rise, and your muscles tense. I was hoping to get a stable baseline with their initial blood draw. We'll have to get the guards to calm them down."

I say, "I didn't see any guards."

"Didn't you see the disc players? The ones who looked like innocent mothers who were harmless?"

I nod.

"They're a lethal force, especially because people underestimate their abilities. Their cover is practicing on the disc course while the kids are in school. But in fact, they're trained killers."

I gulp.

She points a finger at me. "I mean it, don't mess with the disc course ladies. They have special gold frisbees with sharp edges that can take your head off. You've been warned."

She holds out a red plastic cup. "Care for a margarita?"

I'm not sure if she's drugged it, but I take it. "Sure, I'm thirsty, thanks."

Taking a sip of the cold bitter citrus drink with a hint of tequila, I point to the monitor. "What about those women? Where did they come from?"

"Ask Ralph about that. He's in charge of patient enrollment for clinical studies."

She opens a cupboard door and picks up a white phone.

"Jack, tell the Frisbees to get over to the big barn right away. The patients are riled up, and that'll mess with my test results. I need them to calm down. Do whatever it takes. Bribe them. Tell them they'll get an all-expenses-paid trip to Tahiti after this. We need them to sign the consent forms before the trial starts."

She listens and nods to me. "Got it, thanks."

With a shudder, I realize the women in the big barn

are unwilling test subjects. Someone's got to stop that. If I get out, I'll bring the operation down and let those women out.

Scientists in white lab coats file in and take red plastic cups, leaning against the counter or sitting on stools.

A man about five-feet-five with short black hair grins at me. "I'm Ralph. Great job, finding the trap door."

A slender woman with blond curly hair nods and raises her cup. "Well done. I was impressed with your time trial. You broke the record."

"I'm glad you're happy with my performance," I say, "but I shouldn't be here. I need to get back to Cabin Eight and go home. If I want something bad enough, I can be fast. And right now, I'm motivated."

No one says anything. Feet shuffle on the floor. The white-coated scientists look down or stare at the counter. Maybe I hurt their feelings by squashing their congratulations, but I couldn't care less.

I slug back the rest of my drink and go to the sink to fill the cup with water.

As I turn on the faucet, Ms. Goggles rushes over and flips it off.

"Don't drink the tap water. It's not safe. It's specially treated for our tests."

A tall, broad-shouldered man wearing a long, hooded red velvet robe enters the lab and leans against the white wall. When he clears his throat, the others rush over to him. The group mutters about an uprising and unhappy cohort of female volunteers. Ms. Goggles wipes her forehead.

Before they break up their discussion and come back, I hurry to the cupboard where the white phone is hidden. Opening it, I punch in Ned's cell number, the reporter who had been calling me repeatedly and requesting an interview.

Ned picks up right away.

In a low voice, I say, "It's Miranda Diggs. You've got to come to Two Rivers Resort in Millersville. You won't believe what's happening here."

The line goes dead, but I keep talking, in case she can hear me.

"There's wacko underground maybe illegal stuff going on with forced clinical trials on unwilling women patients."

When someone taps me on my shoulder, I turn around.

The poke of a jabbing finger is an accusation without words.

Mr. Red Cape says, "Hang up the phone. It's time for you to leave the lab. See if you can find your way out."

His breath is stale and smells of impatience and coffee with an undertone of pent-up rage. He's staring at me with cold, dark eyes. His face has no expression, as if he's been wiped clean so as to give off no clues of his state of mind.

His thick eyebrows are streaked with gray going every which way. He really should organize that patch of hair or tweeze them or something. He's standing close to me. I can see the open pores of skin on his prominent nose.

What gives me chills is how he wears the hood up of his long red cape, covering his hair and ears. It covers his knees, and he's about six-foot-three. Why is he wearing that? He doesn't fit with the others, who are in white lab coats with pockets.

Spooked by his staring at me, I glance around for Ms. Goggles for reassurance. She's a known entity, and I felt like she was honest with me. I trust her as much as is possible in this strange place. I'll take her with me and make her open an exit door using her eyes for a retina scan.

Ms. Goggles, standing a foot away, crosses her arms and frowns.

Ever since I went into the barn, no one is pleased with me, and that includes me. Most of all, I'm disappointed with myself and how I follow the urge to break rules. That's how the motel fire started. And it's how I ended up in this laboratory.

Ms. Goggles says, "You can't stay long in our lab. This brief stop allowed you to rest before you get on with your challenge."

With a choked chuckle, I say, "I'd like to skip the challenge and just return to Cabin Eight. But not by the cave or tunnel or the trap door."

"Not going to happen," says Mr. Red Robe, stabbing a finger in my direction.

I step back because he's in my bubble of space and I have to wipe his spittle from my cheeks. I want to tell him to say it without spraying it, but I hold back to deliver a more important, powerful request.

"You signed up for the program," he continues, "when you violated posted signs and went in the barn. We can do whatever we like with you."

My throat is dry, even though I drank a margarita. I'm dizzy. The disconnect of this stark, scientific otherworldly environment from my life in Seattle is making my head spin. Or maybe it's from the tequila Ms. Goggles, the master scientist, poured in the blender, along with ice, lime juice, and another unlabeled liquid.

Pointing to Ms. Goggles, I say, "The only way I'll leave the lab is if she goes with me."

Mr. Red Robe glances at her and raises his eyebrows.

"We didn't program in a request like that. It's up to you if you want to take time from your mission-critical experiments." He points to the women in the large barn, who are standing at a barred window, staring out. "And we still need to prepare for our healthy volunteer intake and their initial lab draws."

My heart pounds as I wait, hoping she'll agree to accompany me. I put my hands behind my back and cross my fingers. Say yes, I think. You'll help me escape this surreal closed environment. With your help, I'll run out and free the trapped women in the barn. It's not right they're being held against their will. Someone's got to rescue them, and it might as well be me.

With a smile, I realize that until now, I've been focused on myself and my life and my mistakes and my secret past. Being closed in underground has brought me an awareness that others suffer besides me. Maybe their plight is more important or urgent than my small self-absorbed obsessions, looping endlessly on the fatal mistake I made at summer camp.

"Come on," I say to her. "Just for five or ten minutes. It's chilly in here, and we're closed in. Just walk with me for a bit, and you can come back."

She shrugs. "I could use a short walk." Nodding to Mr. Red Robe, she says, "I'll go with her for five minutes. If I'm not back in ten, call security. But I think this one is harmless."

9

Ms. Goggles and I go down a gray linoleum hallway. My shoes squeak on the hard surface. My only wish is to get out of here alive.

My plan is to open an exit door and run out. I'll pretend I'm curious to see how a retina scan works and ask her to show me. Before I do that, I need to establish a connection with her, so I say, "How long have you worked here?"

"About a year."

"And before that?"

"I was in charge of research and development for a biotechnology company in the Bay Area. I supervised over two hundred scientists. Then Chaos came along with an enticing offer I couldn't pass up. I thought I'd be happier in a rural area." She shrugged. "Hasn't worked out that way though. We've had our challenges here."

"Is Chaos the name of the company running this facility?"

She nods. "Yep, we're a solutions-focused healthcare company. A venture capitalist thought it up."

"Must take big money," I say, "to build a place like this. It's quite a complex, all underground. How do people get out in case of an emergency?"

"Like I said, some of the exit doors don't have locks and lead to stairwells. To get to work, we take the elevators."

To keep her busy while I scope out the facility, I say, "Where do you live? I assume you don't live at the resort?"

She shakes her head. "No way you'd get me to stay overnight in one of those musty cabins. The resort is a cover for our operation. Did they really place a child's red tricycle and one red mitten in Cabin Eight for you to find? I heard it was staged so you'd be a little bit put off by that, and they hoped it might drive you outside. Make you uncomfortable, you know?"

I say, "It worked. It felt like something bad happened there when I saw the one red mitten. So, I went for a walk to clear my head."

"Something did happen in your cabin, but I've been told not to discuss it with you."

Acting on a hunch, I say, "Did it involve the death of a young child? A little girl around four years old?"

Her eyes grow wide. "I can't confirm or deny that."

We stop at a long rectangular window looking into a laboratory. About thirty scientists in blue hazmat suits with the hoods pulled up are wearing goggles, blue gloves, and transparent face shields. Each is standing under a vent hood.

The whole effect looks high-tech, sterile, and industrial. I watch as a man uses a large syringe to draw clear liquid from a vial before squirting it into a series of test tubes.

Wanting to find out more about the place to know what I'm up against, I say, "What are they doing?"

She points. "They're using a pipette to measure and transfer small amounts of our drug in development that will be used in clinical trials. The healthy volunteers you saw in the large barn will each be given an injection. It's a placebo-controlled study, so some participants won't be given the active agent."

I frown. "But don't you think it's wrong to give your drug to those women? It sounds like they didn't agree to be test subjects."

Her jaw clenches. She stares into the lab and doesn't reply.

A few workers glance over at us and raise their eyebrows in a silent question.

She shakes her head at them and looks down at her feet.

I shake a finger at her. "Where are your ethics? Where's your sense of right and wrong?"

She steps closer, pointing back at me. "Really? Is that how you're going to play this? According to my sources, and I was briefed before you wandered into my lab, you're the one who should re-evaluate how you treat people. How have you harmed others? Isn't that the bigger question you're ignoring?"

I swallow hard. My face heats, and I chew on a fingernail that's filthy and chipped from my time in the barn and the tunnel.

With a sigh, I say, "Fine, you're right. I have a reckoning to deal with myself. When I get out of here, I'll take full ownership. But this is a lot bigger, involving unwilling women being forced into a clinical trial. You've got to face it. It's wrong."

My pulse quickens. I'm worked up about what Chaos is doing underground, out of sight of citizen's eyes.

I clench my fists. "You can do something to stop this. You're in a powerful position. You're the lead scientist."

She doesn't meet my eyes and brushes lint off her lab coat.

But I have a feeling I'm getting through to her, so I continue.

"Those women in the barn didn't sign up for this. It's not ethical to go ahead. Call a halt to what you're doing. Stop the project."

Her lips form a thin line. "Nice try, but there's too much at stake here to stop Project Zeno. Too much money is invested, too many investors are counting on a payout, and too many people in the world will need our cure in the coming years. It'll be worth it in the long run. We're taking short-term risks to get the end results. Science doesn't happen overnight, and we're improving the process to pick up the pace."

I snort. "You sound like you're convincing yourself. You've been brainwashed. How did they get to you? By offering a huge bonus when the project is complete?"

"Spot on," she says. "You're observant. Let's keep walking. I only have a few minutes left, then I've got to go back for a staff meeting."

I don't have much time left to take advantage of her, so I say, "Could you at least show me how the retina scanners work? I'm interested in that because it seems incredible that a computer can recognize it."

She eyes me for a moment. "It's an unusual request, but sure. The concept has been around for years. It isn't new, so I'm surprised you're so keen to learn about it. I'll show you when we come to one."

Pointing to two side by side doors, I say, "Where do those lead?"

"A large manufacturing room with an exit door, like you were looking for. It requires a retina scan. I can let you in. Are you interested?"

Thinking it'll lead me to freedom, I say, "Absolutely, yes. Let's go."

10

Ms. Goggles approaches a device mounted on the wall beside the doors. Loud machines rumble on the other side of the wall. I wonder what kind of room I'll be going into. Whatever it's like, it can't be stranger than meeting the wise woman in a cave or the tall red-robed man in the lab.

She leans in and looks into a scanner without blinking. A few seconds later, the doors click open with a loud snick.

She gestures. "You go ahead first. I'll follow."

I push on a bar and open the door. Taking a few steps inside, I enter a sprawling room the size of a football field. Blinded by bright lights, I squint. Grinding machinery disorients me. What's going on in here?

By the time I turn around, the doors are closed.

I rush over and pull on the door.

Nothing happens.

Ms. Goggles left me locked inside.

Pounding on the door, I say, "Aren't you coming with me?"

The door stays shut.

I'm locked in a massive room and must find the exit.

Pivoting in place, I face a thicket of metal machinery emitting a hot engine smell with an undertone of burning rubber. A conveyor belt rolls by, squealing with each turn. Fans hanging from the ceiling rotate, moving warm air.

But what is that on the conveyor belt? I must be seeing things. I go over for a closer look.

On an assembly line are tiny green frogs, each the size of my thumb.

When I lean in to see better, their eyes flick open.

Hairs on the back of my neck stand on end.

What kind of hell have I entered?

Shaking my head, I'm not sure what this place is, or what they're manufacturing. Why would frogs be useful in scientific research?

I take a step back. This is distracting, and I can't lose my focus or dawdle. I've got to find the exit door and get out of here.

Across the football stadium-sized room is a door with a red exit sign blinking above it. The white letters pulse, calling attention to it. The machinery is blocking my path. I'll work my way around the room and go out the exit.

Something pokes my right shoulder blade.

I gasp and spin around.

Before me is a man about five-feet-five with straw-colored hair. He's wearing a white shirt and a purple ball cap with a Chaos logo embroidered in white. His face is flushed, and he's fidgeting with a pen in his shirt pocket.

Adjusting his tortoise-shell rimmed glasses, he says, "What're you doing here?"

I can barely hear him above the noise of the machinery.

"I'm trying to find my way to Cabin Eight."

He smiles. "Oh, you're our test subject in Cabin Eight. Nice to meet you." He offers a hand to shake. "I'm Rufus. Call me Roo, if you like. We're scheduled to be together for the next hour."

Shaking his hand, I sense he's assessing me as if I'm a specimen in a lab. His grasp is warm and firm. From the tension in his jaw, he looks intent on following through with whatever task he was assigned, such as sticking by my side and watching me.

"You can forget your assignment," I say. "I'm in a hurry, and I don't have time to hang around. I came in this room because of the exit door, which I want to use, right now. So, I'll get going. Nice to meet you and all that, but I'm running solo, and I don't need any help."

Nodding, he lets go of my hand and holds my gaze. "That's what they all say. And they come to regret it."

"What?"

He strokes his chin, where a shadow of blond stubble

grows. "They don't understand. The game corporate designed must run as planned. Chaos doesn't take chances or let mistakes happen on our premises."

I cock my head. "What are you talking about? Games running as planned? And what mistakes?"

He leans in close, and I smell his astringent aftershave.

"I mean deaths," he says, locking eyes with me and nodding.

I'm not sure if he's trying to scare me or if he's serious. His wide eyes have a zealot's glaze, so I take a step back and glance around. If I go fast, I should be able to outrun him and get out the exit door before he'll stop me.

Before I make a move to run, he raises a hand.

Out of the shadows, an army of white hazmat-suited workers step forward. They ring the room. My mouth drops open. There must be eighty or more of them, spaced ten feet apart. I'll never slip past them.

Or is there a way?

If I don't try to escape, I'll be ensnared in their game, subjected to an experiment, and I could die.

I wring my hands and calculate the odds. I've got to do something. Any action is better than being passive. I won't collapse in a heap on the cold cement floor.

To Roo, I say, "I want to talk to them. Do you have a megaphone?"

His brows furrow. "Why would you do that? They have strict instructions not to vary the sequence. It's been optimized by the Chaos algorithm. No one messes with that. If you do, you'll lose your job."

With a shrug, I say, "Just get me a megaphone. I'll take it from here."

The edges of his mouth turn up, and he almost smiles. "You've got spirit, and I have to admire that. Be right back."

While he strides away to a dark corner, I cross my fingers that he'll come back and help me. Soon, he returns with a bull horn.

He hands it to me. "You've got five minutes for this, or the lights will go out."

Taking the megaphone, I say to him, "Stop worrying about the schedule. I bet you're a time stickler, aren't you?"

He nods.

"I completely understand. Have a touch of OCD? I do."

"Yep," he says. "It works for me in this position, making sure everything is done according to our high standards."

"I get it, but this might be a moment where we need to try going in a new direction, to be more fluid. You get what I mean?"

He cringes, as if I'm made him uncomfortable. "I get it, but I don't like to step out of my comfort zone."

Smiling at him, I say, "Believe me, I don't either. But this chaotic situation calls for it. Alright, here we go."

Lifting the bull horn, I pull the trigger so my voice will be amplified in the cavernous space.

"Friends, almost neighbors and fellow workers, we gather today to pay homage to Roo, here, who is doing the best job as supervisor that I've ever seen."

He blushes and whispers, "Thanks, but I'm head of manufacturing and a vice president. I'm not a supervisor. It's important to make that distinction, to get their respect."

I clear my throat. "Excuse me, Roo here is VP, and in my book, that means he's a VIP. I think we'd all agree he's a very important person, and he really cares about manufacturing. Do you all agree?"

A few heads nod.

"If you do, clap your hands."

A slight patter of gloved hands follows.

"Feel free to really give it all you've got. This time, show Roo how much you appreciate him. Let's applaud all his careful effort and the hard work and time he puts in to make sure this manufacturing line is running seamlessly. Yay, Roo! Am I right? Let's give him a round of applause."

The sound of clapping and cheering fills the room, overriding the droning machinery.

"Okay, right now, Roo and I are going to walk over together to that exit door on the far side, just to check it out. No harm done. Just a few ambling footsteps, that's all. We'd like you to step aside as we pass and go back to your other duties. Nothing to see here. No breaking news.

Nothing important. Just two people taking a stroll. Does everyone get that?"

Heads nod, including Roo's.

I whisper to him, "Link arms with me. Let's walk around the room. You can point out the highlights of the magnificent machines and the stunning conveyor belt and the little frogs as we go. Ready?"

"Ready," he says with a grin, putting his arm though mine.

11

Gliding around the circumference of the room, workers fall away and go back to whatever they were doing before. Except for ten tall broad-shouldered workers who remain steadfast, as if guarding their posts nearest to the conveyor belt.

"Here," Roo says, "we have the largest underground manufacturing facility in the western United States. Heavy duty industrial service elevators bring equipment and raw materials down and transport the finished product up to the surface. We run it through a kayaking and river rafting company. And your Two Rivers Resort, of course. We have trucks transporting product all day long, and with few residents in the area this far out of Millersville, no one seems to notice. It's a well thought out, efficient and profitable operation."

To keep him engaged and hoping he'll forget he's

going off his precious schedule and helping me escape, I say, "What about the frogs? What're they for? Why are they so small? Are they alive or are they life-like toys?"

He pauses for a moment, observing the conveyor belt.

"It's a trade secret. I'm not at liberty to discuss that with you or anyone else."

"Come on," I say, "I'm right here. I can see them with my own eyes. What harm would it do to tell just one person what's going on here? And what about the strange game you're all playing? It's dangerous, and someone could die. Doesn't that strike you as something to yell about from the rooftops and get the Feds in here to clean house?"

He shakes his head. "How little you know, to say something like that."

"Wait, is the government in on this? Are you doing this for them?"

With a shrug, he says, "No comment."

I frown. "Sounds like this must be a government contract. And the frogs are?"

He leans toward me and in a low voice says, "A synthetic version of an Amazon rainforest frog. It has special characteristics that could be used in warfare."

I don't want him to stop talking, so I make myself look nonchalant, although what he just said rocked me to my core. I've bumbled my way into a secret military operation, being run on contract for the government. An article I read on the internet comes to mind.

"Is this the frog," I say, "where if you ingest scrapings from the skin, you vomit, but then you can see in the dark and run for miles without tiring and not get hungry for two to three days?"

He puts a finger to his lips. "Keep your voice down. Deltorphins from the skin of the Phyllomedusa bicolor have pharmaceutical uses. They're four to six inches from snout to vent, but we found a way to genetically engineer and manufacture smaller versions for mass production."

I blow out a breath while I absorb this information. On the conveyor belts, hundreds of frogs with waxy lime green skin on top and white underbellies look at me with black eyes. They're as trapped as I am in this room.

"Why aren't they hopping around?"

"We reduced the urge to hop. We engineered a more laid-back frog."

A feeling of horror sweeps over me. Ms. Goggles and the white-coated scientists seemed like trustworthy people working to do good in the world, as did Roo when I met him. The women in the barn are unwilling subjects. And the man in the red robe was an outlier, lurking around with his face barely visible behind his raised hood.

Pieces are falling together, and I'm coming to see the facility in a whole new light. Greed is the bedrock of the company called Chaos. The people at the top don't care about people's objections to being corralled in a barn, or the fate of little frogs on an assembly line.

A door opens to the hall where I came in from, and a slight breeze blows past.

Mr. Red Robe strides in, and my stomach knots. He's scowling. Why is he here? I hope I'll be able to get out despite his presence over there, across the room.

As a chill sweeps over me, I shudder. Rubbing my hands for warmth, I say, "I thought you said you could produce the material synthetically. You know the chemical structure of the frog skin, don't you?"

"We do."

"Why would you want to subject real frogs to this when you could do it in a test tube?"

"Management wanted it this way. Said the optics were better for attracting new investors. The green frogs grab people's attention in presentations and on secret site tours for top tier prospects. It's like eye candy. The frogs bring in millions of dollars and pump up our stock."

The horror of what they're doing here makes me flinch, as if he'd slapped me. The frogs look as trapped as I am in this room.

He beams. "Our stock is at an all-time high. If I sold my stock options today, I could buy a waterfront home. I'm waiting for a higher price, then I'll buy my own island."

Something snaps inside me. This isn't right. I must correct this injustice and free the frogs.

I glance around for a button to smack to stop the assembly lines and shut down the conveyor belts. There's one in the center of the room between two gigantic machines. But before I can act, Mr. Red Robe locks eyes with me and shakes his head. He heads my way.

He motions to a worker, who goes over to him. He points at me, and I see his lips move. He's telling them something.

In this moment, I have a choice. I can run out the exit door, ten feet away on my right. Or I can save the frogs. I value my life, but up until now, I've been selfish. I've done nothing for the good of others, not even a pet or a friend, or a stray dog or a cat.

I say to Roo, "Watch me and hold off any attackers. I've got to do this."

Running to a round red button labeled STOP, I smack it with the palm of my hand. The machinery grinds to a halt. The overhead fans stop.

Silence falls in the vast room, broken only by the sound of frogs making their voices known.

Ribbit.

Tiny lime green frogs come alive and wave their arms and legs.

Croaking in a chorus, they rise up.

One follows another out the door Mr. Red Robe propped open when he came in.

Standing on the conveyor belt, I raise my fist and yell, "Go, go! Be free while you can."

Thousands of green frogs hop off the conveyor belts and leap over each other, out of the room.

Mr. Red Robe scowls at me and hustles to the door. He tries to pull it shut but in vain. The doorway and hall are filled with frogs.

The massive surge of frogs is too much for him.

Clawing the air for support, he falls over and disappears beneath a sea of green and white.

I hop down to the floor, ready to run out of this wretched place. But just as I make a break for the exit door, someone grabs my hand from behind.

A woman who smells of lavender and mint whispers, "I'd think twice before you leave. You never know what's on the other side of those doors. It might be worse than what you found in this room."

Wrenching my hands free, I make a break for freedom.

I bang through the exit doors and leave the manufacturing room behind.

12

I stand in a dimly lit space and sniff stale air. It smells of mold. No one has followed me out the exit door, so I hope I haven't made a mistake and plunged into an even worse situation.

They're probably busy inside, trying to corral the hopping frogs. That's why no one chased me. Or is this part of their deluded game, and I've gone according to their predicted plan? I hope not.

I only want to get back to my one-bedroom North Seattle apartment. I'll be so glad when I'm home. I'll clean houses with extra diligence and be thankful I'm not locked in an underground science laboratory and manufacturing facility.

I can barely make out shapes in the weak light, so I shuffle along with my arms out front of me in case there's an obstacle I can't see. I move toward the light.

I smack into a solid block of a person. A standing pillar of muscle is what it feels like.

A man says in a deep voice, "I'd rather you didn't ram into me. I'm here, you see. Right in front of you."

He clicks on a flashlight, aiming it toward the cement floor. A drop of water falls from above and lands by our feet. He's wearing brown cowboy boots, which I bet don't conform to regulation uniform standards in a manufacturing facility. I move my toes around in my running shoes, thankful I'm not barefoot.

"What're you doing here?" I say, reaching for the torch. "Can I borrow that?"

"Don't be greedy. We can share it. Unless you don't want to get out of here, that is."

I nod but then realize he might not see my expression. His straw hat has wide brim, and it's pulled down over his eyes. He's wearing a red shirt under a long tan trench coat.

"I definitely want to get out of here," I say, "and go back above ground to Cabin Eight. I've got to go home. My mother must be missing me by now."

He says, "Nice, you're close to your family."

"Not really, just my mom. That's the extent of our family now. But what are you doing here?"

"I was assigned to spot you and make sure you didn't run into trouble. From here on out, we're a team. Team Trouble, that's our nickname." He chuckles. "I like what you did in there, letting loose the frogs to take over the plant. It'll take them a long time to get that under control."

"I hope they never do. I don't think anyone should be experimenting with those frogs. Or with the women in the barn. There's a heck of a lot that's going on wrong here. How can you stand being part of it?"

"I'm just a gun for hire, doing what they tell me to do. It doesn't pay to have a conscience." He flashes the light up, illuminating a stairway. "Shall we go up and see what's at the top?"

"Of course. That's where I'm headed, and you can come along."

Striding up the stairs, I'm out of breath by the second landing. We were farther down than I'd thought. Pausing and panting, I say, "Why are you helping me? If you hadn't been there, I'd be fumbling around in the dark."

"I'm sure you would've figured out a way. Where's your phone? You could've used the flashlight app."

"I lost it when I fell down a tunnel."

"So, I bet you learned it doesn't pay to get nosy and poke into other people's businesses or barns. Is that right?"

"Maybe not. Let's get going again."

Gripping a metal railing, I pull myself up, one step at a time. My muscles are weak, and I'm exhausted. This whole adventure has taken a toll on me. I'm disoriented from being underground and feeling out of control.

About five flights up, I stop again, wheezing and out of breath.

"Take your time," he says. "We're not in a hurry. They

allotted forty-five minutes for this aspect of the game. No need to rush at a breakneck pace."

Facing him, spittle flies from my mouth when I say, "I'm so sick of hearing about that stupid game. We're not pawns on a board. We're people with lives of our own and decisions to make. A company just can't come in and control us."

"Calm down. I'm just trying to make a buck here. I'm not in charge of the evil empire."

I clench my fists. "Isn't everyone participating helping it run? Without the cogs turning, wouldn't it grind to a halt? And by the way, I absolutely hate it when someone tells me to calm down. Hearing it makes my blood pressure spike."

He holds up his hands. "Sorry to upset you. Let's keep going."

Two floors up, I stop on a landing. "How much farther?"

"Who am I? The magic answer guy? I'm not supposed to provide clues. You have to find them for yourself."

Looking up, I let out a scream, a long wailing shriek of frustration.

"Feel better?" he says.

My stomach rumbles.

"I'm tired, I'm hungry, and I want to go home."

"Not much longer now. Imagine a beer ahead when you get to the top."

"I'm more of a margarita drinker." The color of a

margarita reminds me of the scene we left behind. "Those poor green frogs."

"I know, but you set them free. Maybe they'll shut down the manufacturing operation after what you did. Or at least pause production for cleaning and repairs. Might as well."

Climbing the stairs, my thigh muscles ache. My knees creak. I'm out of shape.

I say, "What do you do for a living?"

"Nothing much. I work security odd jobs here and there. Pays the bills and puts my son through college."

I stop to catch my breath. The light up ahead is getting stronger, coming from a window in a door at the top of the stairs. My guess is it will open inside the complex, which is not what I want.

"You don't look old enough to have a son in college," I say.

He shrugs. "Had him when I was young, and I wouldn't change a thing. Makes working worth it and life better all around."

"Sounds appealing, but I wouldn't know about that. What's he majoring in?"

"Finance. It'll bore the socks off him when he's working, but he wants a steady paycheck. He didn't like it when we had to eat dandelion soup for dinner when I was between jobs."

"I can understand that. What's up ahead? Do you know?"

"I don't. I was instructed to escort you up the staircase. Then we'll part ways. I guess they want to see what you'll do next."

I groan. "I'm fed up with this game. I didn't sign up to be a test case or have my choices controlled and monitored."

He tilts his head. "They picked you for some reason. From what I hear, you're the first player to run the chaos game this far. You must be pretty special or something."

I shrug. "I'm nobody special. I'm an average person with an average family who has made mistakes and is getting her life back together. Or so I'd hoped before I came here."

"I've also heard whispers about Subject 1, which is you I suspect, and how you took a quiz administered online through social media. You ranked the highest in what they were looking for."

Rolling my eyes as I take a step up the last flight, I say, "I knew I shouldn't have clicked on that quiz. It said, 'Which are you most like? An apple, a pear, or a crocodile?' I filled it out and look what happened. I ended up here." With a snort, I say, "Maybe they were looking for messed up people with dark pasts who wanted to start over."

"Maybe," he says.

I've appreciated his company on this stage of my journey, so I say, "If I don't see you again, take care."

"You too. Whatever they throw at you, I'm sure you can take it."

"Thanks, I hope so." My voice wavers as I say, "Do you know anything else they have planned?"

"No, I don't. Not even a whiff of rumor about it. I'm low in the hierarchy here."

Blowing out a breath, I envision my return home, and it gives me hope. I've come through hard times in the past. I can do this.

At the top of the stairs, I grasp a cold metal door handle and tug it open. I don't know what I'll find on the other side. But whatever it is, it can't be worse than what I saw downstairs. At least I'm closer to ground level now with a better chance of leaping in my car and leaving this dangerous, senseless game far behind.

13

I'm temporarily blinded by a harsh bright light in the hallway and put up a hand to shield my eyes. About fifteen feet away is an older woman with loose, long gray hair. She's standing with her hands in her white lab coat pockets. She's almost six feet tall and wearing black yoga pants with yellow running shoes. She frowns and studies me closely, like I'm a bug under a microscope.

"Hi." I wave. I'm intimidated by her presence. Without her saying a word, I get the feeling she's smart and calm and a much better person than I am or ever will be.

"You're late," she says, tapping a black smart watch on her wrist. "I've got better things to do than wait around for you to show up. Come on then, don't just stand there. Let's get going."

I stand there, open mouthed, taking it all in. My feet

don't move. This last bit is almost too much for me to take. I'm not sure I have the stamina to keep going. When will this game end?

I turn to say something to the straw-hatted man in the trench coat who went up the stairs with me, but he's gone. He must've taken the stairs back down. It was too much to hope for support in this mess, anyway. I'm on my own once again.

She points to a spot on the floor by her feet and speaks slowly.

"Get going. Your time is below average, and you're lagging behind our projected estimates. I don't want you to bring down the average. Statistics matter. Get over here now, and fast."

I nod and force myself forward, taking one step at a time under the bright lights. Here I go, marching toward what may be my death. I could end up like the frogs on an assembly line. They could use my blood or DNA for a scientific experiment.

"Don't clone me," I blurt out. "It wouldn't be worth it. Other people would be far better to have duplicates or triplicates of. The world doesn't need another me around."

I'm blathering on and running my mouth because I'm stone-cold nervous. I need to use a bathroom, and I'm hungry and thirsty. This is not how I wanted to spend my holiday.

She chuckles. "Don't worry, we're not going to do that

to you. Not yet. But I would like you to step into my workspace for a brief test."

Standing in front of her, I hold up my hands.

"No tests, no way, no thanks. I'm not a fan of needles, never have been."

"Come with me," she says, guiding me by the elbow with a firm grip into a windowed room with microscopes on the counters. A sliding glass door opens to an enclosure with-tall clear cylinders containing a cloudy white liquid.

I point at them. "What's in those containers?"

She grins. "We're growing cells. I have the best track record in the facility. For some reason, the cells multiply faster for me."

She stands with her hands on her hips, looking relaxed and confident.

She's a master of her craft, which is what I'd like to be one day. The trouble is, I haven't identified what I'd like to do yet beyond helping my mother with her business. But it would be a relief to leave house cleaning behind. Scrubbing floors hurts my knees. Other people's trash is gross. And don't get me started on stains on the bedsheets.

Gesturing to the cylinders, she says, "We scale up and turn them into medicines."

She wiggles her fingers and comes closer.

Her eyes grow wide as she says, "It's spooky business."

When I gasp and cover my mouth, she chuckles. "Don't worry about it. If I went into an explanation, it'd sound like a bunch of scientific mumbo jumbo. Now let's get started on your project."

Wanting details so I can pass them onto the reporter, I say, "Don't hold back. I'm interested. Tell me more."

She laughs and slips a hospital band around my wrist. "No distracting me with chatter. I've got to fulfill my duties and finish my assigned task."

"And what exactly is that?"

When she doesn't answer, I examine the plastic identification band and read: Subject 1, Chaos Game 100x7, Experiment 1a.

My stomach sinks. I can't be part of an experiment.

When I try to tug it off, she pats my hand.

"Compliance is best, Subject 1. Let's begin. Sit down, and I'll draw your blood."

My heart thumps as I look around for a way to escape.

She's standing in front of the doorway, blocking it, and I don't see any other exits.

"I need to use the restroom," I say, "and I'm thirsty. I'm dehydrated, so it won't be an easy blood draw unless I drink water and warm up first." I know this bit of information because my mother mentioned it last week when she went to the doctor's office.

She sighs. "Fine. We'll go take care of that. But you're not getting out of my sight."

I do my best to look casual. "Sure, no big deal. Let's go."

She guides me into an adjacent bathroom and stands outside my stall.

I'm so rattled all I can do is sit, clenched up tight on the plastic toilet seat.

My muscles won't relax.

"I don't hear anything happening," she says.

She's close enough I see her tapping her toes. Those yellow shoes are a bit much, but when I get out of here, I'll look into buying a pair. They certainly make a statement.

Clearing my throat, I say, "I have a shy bladder."

Her shoes squeak as she pivots to face me from outside the stall. "What are you talking about? That's all a myth."

"No, really, I've always been like this. I can't use the facilities if someone is in here with me. Especially like now, if you're watching and listening. I need privacy or I can't do my business."

"Good grief. Fine, I'll leave you to it and be back in a few minutes. But don't take too long. We have ten vials to fill with your blood and then we have other experiments to conduct."

My head is light, and the room twirls. I'm dizzy, so I lean down and put my head between my knees while still on the can.

I mumble to myself, "I can't do this. I don't like needles. Don't take my blood. Let me go home."

Footsteps cross the hallway floor. The door hinges groan.

"No excuses. Hurry up and get on with it. I'm waiting out here for you."

Glancing around, I spot a window above the toilet.

My pulse races. This is my chance. I'm finally alone.

As quick as I can, I do my business and wipe myself, pulling up my pants.

I smile. Subject 1 is about to leave the building. Nothing to see here. Just a very afraid young woman running for her life.

I step onto the toilet and steady myself, gripping the windowsill. I've got to get away from these crazed people who are messing with human and amphibian lives. They've taken one measure of corporate power motivated by greed, blended in high tech gaming expertise, and stirred in scientific genius. Chaos is a toxic formula.

The bathroom door opens.

I swing down into a sitting position and hum a tune for cover.

"Are you finished?" she says in a harsh tone. "I have work to do."

"La dee da," I sing. "I always sing on the toilet. It helps me relax."

"Alright then, but get busy and finish up, or I'll have to drag you back to the lab."

"No need for that." I hum a few bars of 'Over the Rainbow' to distract her. "It won't be long. I'll come out when I'm done."

"When you're finished, you mean. Done is for chickens cooking in the roaster."

I roll my eyes, but she can't see me. As far as I know, she doesn't have x-ray vision. Or have they developed that too, along with little green frogs and cures for maladies?

To get her to leave, I say, "I need to be alone."

"Three more minutes. That's all I'm giving you."

"Kay."

The door closes with a thud.

Jumping on the toilet seat, I turn the latch and push open the window. Maybe they installed it for ventilation, in case someone did something super stinky in here. Wrapping my fingers over the window frame, I pull myself up.

I squeeze through the two-foot-wide opening and crawl out on my belly.

I stand and look around.

I'm in a five-foot-wide open-air shaft that goes up one story.

Above me is gray sky.

It's so far away.

Fresh air wafts down, bringing a smell of moisture.

I'm outside, but I'm trapped.

14

I cross my arms in the air shaft and hang my head and cry. My shoulders shudder. Tears run down my cheeks. I'm so tired of this stupid game. How long can I keep this up?

Hearing voices snaps my attention back to my dire situation. I don't have time for self-pity. Book that on the calendar for next week or next month or never.

I bend and quietly close the window to the bathroom. They won't be fooled long, if at all. I've got to figure out what to do next.

A thought occurs to me. In the game they designed, and for what purpose I have no idea, I'm a pawn on a chessboard. What if they hid clues for me to discover so I could escape? Fat chance of that, but I might as well look.

I wipe my nose with the back of my hand and take a deep breath, assessing the situation. This area might have been designed to give maintenance workers access. There has to be a way out.

Craning my neck, I stare at the bare, boxed-in walls. I spot bronze metal rods in the wall at two-foot intervals going up to the top. But that won't help me, because I'm not a rock climber or a risk taker. I'm just an ordinary rebel with a butterfly tattoo on my left cheek. If I see a posted rule, I want to break it, like burning the pages from my diary despite a sign saying No Open Flames.

Before this, I thought I was special. Mainstream people with regular ho-hum brain-freeze jobs had to conform, but I was free to do what I liked. Now I'm paying the price for ignoring a No Trespassing sign and wandering into a barn. My rebelling made me into Subject One.

The voices grow louder.

My heart beats faster.

People are coming to get me, and I'm in a cramped, confined space.

I don't want to climb and pull myself up by those hand holds.

If one came off the wall or broke under my weight, I'd tumble to my death.

But I don't see an elevator or a fairy godmother. There's just me and those hand holds. So up I must go.

I reach up and grasp a cold metal rod.

With a click, it slides out of the wall. Behind the rod is a step.

Other steps come out, one by one, making a mechanical whirring noise.

"Going up," a disembodied woman's voice says.

"Keep quiet," I say in a low voice, "I don't want them to find me."

"As you wish."

I swiftly make my way up and pause halfway to catch my breath.

My thigh muscles are screaming.

My fingers ache.

I'm not used to exerting myself like this.

"Going down," the voice says.

The steps I'm holding onto and standing on start to move toward the wall.

"No," I hiss. "I just stopped for a moment."

The metal steps are slowly disappearing into the mysterious wall.

"Stop," I say in a breathless voice.

I don't want to fall. It's a long way down.

A beeping noise goes off.

A red button labeled "Push me" emerges from the wall.

Before my fingers are squashed, I smack the button.

The steps grind to a halt.

A portion of the wall slides open in front of me, revealing an air duct.

"Step in," a recorded voice says.

Taking a moment to let my forehead rest on the metal

rod, I wonder if I can make the leap from the step into that duct. I have no idea where it goes. Do I even want to climb in there?

The sound of clapping fills my ears.

Down below, the woman in the white lab coat who wanted to draw my blood waves and says with a smile, "You can do this! We picked you, and we know you're up to the task."

"What if I don't want to play?"

She lets out a belly laugh and rests her hand on her stomach.

"Then you'll be stuck there. We'll scrape you up when you fall down. We'll cremate your remains and sprinkle your ashes in the Salish Sea."

I cringe, tasting bitter bile. I'm not ready for death, not at their hands, during this monstrous game they devised.

"I want to live," I shout, raising a clenched fist.

Adrenaline courses through my body, like a tap has been turned on.

With newfound strength, I scramble across a foot-wide gap.

I stumble as I land in the air duct and almost fall down below into the abyss. My hands are slick with sweat. My muscles are trembling.

"We knew you could do it," the gray-haired scientist calls.

From up here, she's small. But her wide grin and stance with feet apart makes her look like a giant, which she is in her field, from what she said. When I get out of here, I'd like to read some of her scientific articles.

I cup my hands and say, "What's your name? I forgot to ask."

"Mildred, Mildred Redding."

A rope drops from the ceiling, and she ties a plastic shopping bag to it. "Up."

The package rises to the air duct and stops.

"We thought you might be hungry," she says.

With a smile, I wave and say, "I am, thanks."

I pull the rope over, untie the bag and open it. Inside is a bruised banana, a tin of sardines and a hard roll with sea salt sprinkled on top.

"Not to be picky, but I hate sardines," I call down.

My voice echoes in the metal air duct.

"I know. That's why we gave you that. Buck up and make do. It's time for an attitude change."

With a snort, I shake my head. I've entered a weird world where these people know everything about me. Then I reconsider. I have one secret they haven't mentioned. They don't know about the fateful day at summer camp.

My mouth waters. I bite into the hard roll and chew, appreciating each morsel. It tastes of nutmeg and walnuts and rye flour. A strange combination, but it works.

When I pull at the sardine can's metal tab, it snaps off without opening the tin. I need protein, and I have no way to open it without a can opener. Just as well. It would've been oily and the smell of fish overpowering.

Taking a chance that the scientist is still down below, I say, "I can't open the tin."

"Find a way," Mildred says. "Or keep it to bargain with."

With a groan, I say, "I don't want to bargain. I want to go home."

"I'm leaving now. Look for the note."

"Goodbye, Mildred."

"Goodbye, and you'd better get going. Your time is about to run out. You don't want to be caught in the wrong place."

15

I bite my lip and think about what Mildred the scientist said. My time is running out, and I'm in the wrong place. I don't want to die, not here, not now and not today.

A pinging noise distracts me. It's coming from far away in the facility.

I open the plastic shopping bag and pluck out a cream-colored piece of Chaos corporate letterhead stationery. It's a printed letter. Now what, I wonder. And just exactly who is running this creepy show? I want to go to the top and complain about how this place is run. I'll tell them to stop experimenting with unwilling humans.

It says, "Don't go straight, but turn left. Stop thinking about going home or returning to Cabin Eight. Be where you are for best results."

I roll my eyes at what strikes me as a bunch of platitudes from a self-help book. Folding the page, I cram it in my pocket in case I'll need it later. I carry the plastic bag and crawl on my hands and knees through the narrow air duct. My breath is shallow, as if I'm being squeezed to death in the metal tube.

I swallow and sigh. How did I end up here of all places? And what lies ahead? What or who is waiting me on the other end?

Groping along on my hands and knees, the metal tube vibrates with a high-pitched ringing. The reverberation surrounds me.

I stop, clapping my filthy hands over my ears. My wrists and shoulders and knees ache. I should've climbed faster and been more agile. I should've scaled the air shaft to the top and run for it. That's the story of my life, lugging around a pack of regrets.

Sweat trickles down my back. The noise stops, and I take my hands off my ears. My fingers form dim shapes. I can't make out much in the dark tube.

Creeping ahead a few feet, I stop and listen. I hear drops of water falling. Far off, a fan whirs.

Dust tickles my nose. I sneeze three times, like I always do.

A glowing light appears ahead.

In a low voice, a woman says, "Who goes there?"

My stomach knots.

I'm not sure who she is, but I'm about to find out.

"I'm just passing through," I say, as if it's an everyday occurrence. "I'm trying to get out of here."

"That's what they all say. What's your name?"

"Miranda Diggs."

"From?"

"Seattle."

"No, I mean which cabin?"

My voice ends in a question when I say, "Cabin Eight?"

My confidence is ebbing. The situation is surreal. I'm talking with a stranger in a metal air duct. Beam me home, please. I'll do whatever it takes. Somehow, I've got to figure out a way to get out of here.

Thinking of Seattle reminds me of my mom. When I was growing up, we'd eat popcorn for dinner on Sundays and watch old Star Trek episodes. Mom, I'm coming home, don't worry. For your sake, I won't die in this duct.

The woman in front of me is about forty and wearing a headlamp strapped on her forehead by a yellow-striped band. I wish I hadn't left mine in the lab. Her brown hair is cut shoulder-length. Her ears are huge. Diamond studs in the cartilage sparkle when she moves. She's wearing blue braces.

She pulls out her phone and types a text. The clicking makes a satisfying sound as she taps out a message. A hunger to cradle a phone rises within me. I miss my device.

She pockets the phone. "All right, Cabin Eight, I was waiting for you. About time you checked in. There's a fifteen-hundred-dollar surcharge if you're more than thirty minutes late. Keep that in mind as you move down the line."

"That's a load of B.S. if I ever heard it."

She shrugs and looks me over. "Policies and procedures. Out of my hands. Take it to the next level if you don't like it."

"I just may do that. Who is in charge?"

"I'm not allowed to divulge that."

Reaching out, I say, "Could I use your phone? I lost mine."

She shakes her head. "Nope. It's your fault. You should've taken care of it. Let's go."

She turns and crawls away.

Blowing out a breath, I don't want to follow her. What if she traps me or leads me into danger? With a shudder, I imagine my worst fear slithering down the duct, ready to wrap around my torso and strangle me. I gulp. Please, no snakes, whatever happens. And especially no boa constrictors.

I cringe, realizing they have private intel on me. They may already be aware of my fear of snakes. Oh lord, I hope they don't discover that tidbit. I've never mentioned it on social media, so I bet I'm safe.

She glances back with an exasperated look. "What's keeping you? Come on."

Her headlamp blinds me, and I shield my eyes.

"I'm not used to this kind of thing. Can we stop whatever we're doing, and I'll leave? I won't say a thing to anyone, I promise."

I've just told a lie, which I rarely do. But this instance called for it. When I'm away from Chaos and Two Rivers Resort, I'll call the reporter and report the clinical trial violations to the FDA.

When we come to a fork in the duct, she stops.

"We go this way," she says, pointing straight ahead.

"No, I can't. I'm supposed to go left."

"Who told you that?"

I pull out the piece of paper and hand it to her. "It's on letterhead, so it must be official."

She pokes a finger at it. Her knuckles are knotty and enlarged. She must have arthritis. Crawling on her hands must be painful for her.

"Look at the date. It's marked as of last month. New orders came down yesterday. Didn't Mildred tell you to disregard this?"

I smack my forehead. "Oh, my goodness, would you please stop messing with my mind? I just want to get out of here. I'm going left, no matter what you say. Mildred seemed like someone I could trust. I don't think she would've misled me."

"Who am I? French toast slathered in ketchup and mustard? I'm insulted you'd believe her over me." She squints. "What is it about me that makes you not trust me? Is it the headlamp?"

I shake my head.

"Or the studs in my ears?"

"Nope, that's not it."

"The braces," she says, her eyes lighting up. "I knew I shouldn't have gone for the blue color."

With a shrug, I say, "It's more of your gruff tone."

She frowns. "Gruff?"

"Yeah, your initial tone upon meeting me was a bit harsh. You could warm it up some. Make a friendlier presentation. Maybe smile once in a while."

She bites her lip. "I am sick of being told to smile more." Then she cocks her head. "But my last 360 performance review did say I could be less cold and clinical when offering feedback to my team. So, I'll consider what you said. Now, I can't let you go in a different direction than where I'm heading. You decide. It's straight ahead, or you can sit here and starve to death. You'll shrivel up. You'll be desiccated and turn into a dust ball. No one will find you."

Shaking my head, I say, "I'm going left, no matter what you say."

"Are you sure?" She arches her eyebrows. "There are snakes to the left. Boa constrictors, I've heard. I wouldn't try it, not if you paid me a trillion dollars."

A chill runs up my spine. I squint, trying to recall if I checked the box for fear of snakes on that online survey. Was there a question about what I most feared? Yes, I think there was, and like an idiot, I filled in the blank with the words boa constrictor.

A slight smile hovers at the edges of her mouth, making me wonder if she's joking with me. This could be a test of my stamina and will power. Do I have the courage to take a duct on the left and face possible snakes? Or will I wimp out and follow her straight ahead?

I trust my gut. My instincts tell me to turn left. It may lead to my sudden death, but I must take it.

A note taped to the air duct on the left catches my eye.

"Take the left one. Wishing you all the best, Mildred."

"I'm going left," I say, pointing. "Mildred's note there confirms it for me."

The woman scowls and snatches the note, ripping it to shreds.

"Mildred is always messing with my projects. This is the last time she'll get away with that."

"Well, thanks for your help, getting me this far. I hope your next performance review is five out of five stars."

She half-smiles. "That's not how they're rated, but whatever. Thanks, kid. You take care of yourself. I'm going back to work, and you're on your own."

"What's your regular job?"

"I'm in charge of supply chain logistics." She beams. "It's an important position, very complicated sorting out issues, but someone's got to do it."

Holding out my hand, we shake.

"My name is Beverly, if we ever run into each other again."

"Thanks, Beverly. It's been a pleasure."

"Take care, Cabin Eight." She pulls out her phone. "Or should I say Subject One?"

I shudder.

She says, "You've got five minutes to make it through. Starting, now."

I scramble ahead down the duct, my pulse thumping in my ears. I could use five cups of coffee now and a thin crust pizza with olives, artichoke hearts and basil. My arms tremble from exertion, and I stop, panting in place to catch my breath.

Beverly says, "You'd better get going. Or the snakes will multiply. We have enough in cages, so we can always send more in."

She cackles, issuing an evil laugh.

Cringing, I charge ahead on my hands and knees, moaning and in pain.

My palms throb. My fingers hurt. Every bone aches.

Was she serious about the snakes?

And what else did I fill in on the survey about what makes me panic? I bite my lower lip. I may have mentioned my fear of being trapped in a room when a water main is backing up and there are no windows. Uh oh.

My hands grow cold. I fed them fodder that may lead to my demise. I gave them the blueprint for how to freak me out. I must not panic. Remain calm. Keep crawling.

When my fingers touch pellets of what smells like rodent dung, I gag.

My breath is shallow. My hands shake. My mind reels, imagining snakes in the duct moving toward me. Slithering quietly in my direction.

My shoulders rise around my neck, and I put my hands together. Anything but that.

The duct reverberates with a high-pitched sound, like someone hitting a tuning fork. The ringing in my ears grows louder. I crawl ahead, but I'm not sure how much longer I can hold out.

16

The air duct is dark. My heart beats fast, and I'm perspiring. I fumble and grope. Moving forward, I'm afraid of what I might find.

Something slithers toward me, and my eyes open wide. It must be my imagination. My chest constricts. Whatever they're doing is working. They're squeezing the life out of me.

If only I'd stayed in the cabin for a cup of coffee, instead of poking my nose in a barn where I didn't belong. I swear, when I get out, I'm going to respect rules in a whole new way.

In a wavering voice, I say, "Who's there?"

Swish. Slither.

Fear drips off me in beads of sweat. But I keep going, moving ahead. I wonder if the reporter got my phone call, and if she'll do anything about it.

I imagine my mother blasting into the facility with a truck and coming to my rescue. But she's not coming to help, so I'll emulate her and tap my inner strength. If I can get my hands on a truck, I'll break out of the compound.

My hand lands on a rubber-like cylindrical shape.

I shriek.

"What is this?" I scream, hurrying past. "Let me out. I don't want to play this game."

Hustling along, I bang my knees against the duct and nick my hands in haste. I don't care if I get hurt. I only want to escape.

Swish, shush, slither.

Bile rises in my throat.

Move. Get going. I don't have time to throw up. Don't stop.

As I crawl down the duct, going as fast as I can, the snake-like noises cease behind me. Did I leave whatever it was behind? I hope so.

My body trembles. Cuts in my palms smart. The air duct bends, and I follow the curve.

It ends high above a vast room.

My mouth hangs open, and I gape at the bare, empty concrete space.

Is there a way out?

Lights come on below with a clicking sound, giving me enough light to spot a ladder leading down.

I jerk my head, examining the space for exits, but only see smooth stone walls.

The ladder is my only move, unless I turn around and go back, facing writhing snakes. Imagining a bundle of slithering snakes crawling over me makes me shudder. I rub my arms and ponder what to do next.

Gritting my teeth, I decide Chaos won't outwit me today. I'll show them. I'll survive their wretched game. I'll confound them by remaining cool and calm.

My mother comes to mind. If she were here, she'd be proud of how I'm not blubbering like a baby but fighting to get out from this place. As a kid, I was terrified when a clown came up to me at a birthday party. I screamed and hid under a table. My mom came over and coaxed me out, patting me on the back and telling me to face my fears.

We held hands and went over to the clown. I trembled as I introduced myself. When he bent down and told me who he was, he wasn't as scary. He was just Jessica's dad, dressed up in a clown suit. When and if I emerge from this river of horror, I'll thank my mom for teaching me to carry on, no matter what.

"If you were here," I whisper, "you'd be cheering me on. Thanks, Mom. I'll make you proud."

I grab hold of a rung and swing my legs onto the ladder. This is it. I'm going down. This room is the only place to go next.

As I take a step down, a deep fury rises up inside me. They're violating my rights. How dare they limit my choices and control where I go? They'll regret this. When

I get out, I'll report them. I'll rain hellfire and fury on the entire facility.

Taking a deep breath, I yell, "Go stuff yourselves in a test tube for all I care. I'm not playing your crappy game anymore."

The squeak of a hinge draws my attention to a hidden door in the wall.

Three feet away, a hidden door creaks open.

My heart thuds.

Who or what is coming?

A six-foot-tall clown walks out, and I scream at the top of my lungs.

My legs spasm. My hands turn sweaty, but I hold on. I shouldn't have written in the survey that I was afraid of clowns.

Ten feet below me, a cement slab floor waits, but I refuse to give up and die.

The clown comes over and puts his face near mine. He blinks and opens his eyes wide. He's wearing thick black eyeliner and a red rubber nose. His pointed red cowboy boots are an inch from my face. The smell of his white face paint and sandalwood aftershave makes me feel sick.

Squirming on the ladder, I want to throw up.

"How are we today?" he says, raising his red-painted eyebrows. "A little fed up with the whole thing?"

He rests a veined hand on the metal ladder and jiggles it. "Shall I push this over? What do you think?" His voice echoes in the open industrial space.

Holding on tight, I gasp. Maybe a snake will come out of the air duct behind him and take a big bite of his butt.

He flashes his teeth in a wide cruel smile. He straightens up and says in a loud voice, "I'm not at all like Jessica's dad, am I?"

Quick as a lightning strike, he reaches for the ladder.

"Hell, no," I shout, scrambling down with newfound strength.

Imitating what I saw in a movie once, I put my hands and feet on the outside and slide down to the bottom.

I shake a fist at him.

"Take that, you wind bag! You don't scare me."

"Oh, I don't, do I? Watch this."

He pulls a gun out of his pocket.

With a flash of light, a red flare flies past, slamming into the floor near my feet.

I jerk and skitter away. My eyes water. The acrid air makes me cough.

He claps.

"You're quite the adversary," he says. "Our predictions were wrong. You're not the woe-is-me coward we expected."

I put my hands on my hips and snarl, "I'll never be a coward."

He strokes his orange beard. "I can see we need to adjust our statistical model. Our algorithm is off. You shouldn't have gotten this far. Did you have trauma when you were young?"

I screw up my face. What is he talking about? This is out of left field, even in this place.

"No. I had a fine time growing up. My mother was great. Why?"

"Our studies indicated creative types are often driven by loss. Usually something traumatic, often tragic, occurred by age fourteen. What did we miss?" He nods. "I know. We failed to include in our calculations your dreary incident at summer camp."

Frowning, I say, "I wouldn't call it an incident or dreary. That makes light of a death. Especially of someone so young, and someone who was my friend."

Tears wet my cheeks. His words sucker punched me. If only I had that day to do over.

He nods. "I knew it. We should've weighted your early years to account for that loss. It couldn't have been easy to witness a death? First-hand? Was it? Tell me all about it."

The hairs on my arms stand on end. He's getting too close to the truth, and one I avoid at all costs. I'm not even sure why I'm standing here talking to him. It's as if I'm mesmerized by the topic he brought up. I've forgotten my mission is to escape.

Where is that snake? I want it to come out now and coil around his body that's built like a telephone pole.

Furrowing my brow, I say, "Back off. I don't want to talk about it."

"We'll talk about it in the lab later. We'll monitor your

pulse and oxygen levels while we administer tests and ask a series of questions."

I shake my head. "Nope, I'm not doing that. I'm getting out of here and going home. The only good that came of this is I never realized how great my life was until now."

When he cackles, fiendish laughter bounces off the walls.

Spit flies and sprays my cheeks when he says, "You think you can refuse, but it's not an option. You entered at your own risk and ignored posted warnings. You'll give us all the information we seek at any cost. You'll help us improve our model, whether you like it or not."

I grasp the ladder to move it away from the wall. I want to stow it in case I'll need it later. He's creepy and deluded, and he has a cruel streak. I don't want him to hop down the steps and hurt me.

Metal rattles. The ladder jiggles. He pulls on one end, and I hold on to the other.

He snatches it up and brandishes it with both hands before setting it down.

"You thought you could outsmart me, but you can't. I've got a genius IQ. Far higher than yours, I bet."

"Listen, Mr. Rude Red Boots, no need to be snobby about it. We've all got our strengths and weaknesses. It's not a good look if you brag about how smart you are. I bet you're in the Mensa Club, am I right?"

"It's not a club, it a society. I can't talk about it with you. Only if you're a member."

"Well, you can take your secret society and shove it out the tunnel you came in through. If you're Mensa, I'm Wenza, the mighty warrior who overcomes all odds."

He looks confused, so I say, "Fine, I'm Wonder Woman. Just watch me, and see what I can do. I'm going to escape."

He holds up an index finger. "We have one last test for you. Think about what you wrote on your survey. We've got a little surprise in store."

He laughs and puts his hands in the air. "Can she get out of this next test? I fear not."

I cover my ears to block his macabre cackling. He's off his rocker and needs help. He sounds like he'd be happy if I died in this bare room. But whatever they dish out, I'll show them.

Just then, a fat tan snake with dark markings slithers out of the air duct. It moves toward him.

Oh, my goodness. My jaw drops open. I hope it won't find its way down to me.

He snatches it up. Holding it by the jaws, he waves it at me. The tongue flicks out.

"Want to take a closer look? I can throw it down if you like."

I stand with my legs apart and clench my fists. A firm resolve fills me. He's trying to frighten me, but it won't work. I've put on a suit of emotional armor.

"I can take whatever you throw at me. Go ahead, try it."

"That's no fun," he says, taking the snake and tossing it through the hidden door.

He turns back to me and shakes a finger.

"Now we'll see what you're made of. Can you make it? Maybe not."

He leaves and closes the door.

Water trickles into the room where I'm standing. I look around for an exit and see none. I'm stranded without a ladder to climb out.

The trickle becomes a flood, rushing in and swirling around my feet. I don't see a door or a window. I've got to figure this game out before they kill me.

17

Water rushes into the room. The water level rises, submerging my feet and ankles. It smells like sewage. The foul odor makes me cough.

I recall a woman in Seattle years ago who couldn't open her basement door or window when water rushed in from a broken sewer line. What a horrible way to meet an early death. But I have no intention of doing that today.

My muscles tense as I search for a way out. The clown mentioned this was my final test. But he might have been messing with my mind.

Sloshing through fetid water in what looks like forty-foot room, I run my fingers along the wall. I'm searching for a crack to indicate a hidden opening, but to no avail. The walls are smooth and dry, although they won't remain that way for long.

Water licks at my calves. It's coming in through a three-inch-wide black pipe across the room. I wade over there and breathe through my mouth. No amount of perfume or rose petals or burning sage could overpower the smell in this room. The Chaos people are clever and thought of every angle to unhinge me.

I reach into the murky water and yank on the black pipe, hoping to dislodge it. It won't budge. I take the plastic shopping bag with the sardine can and banana peel and bend down, stuffing the bag and its contents into the opening of the pipe.

Water keeps gushing out. The only other weapon I have is my clothing. I pull off my shirt and jam it into the pipe, hoping to plug it up. But the water keeps flowing.

My breathing is shallow. My body is heavy. I'm exhausted, depleted, and running on reserves.

As I lean against the wall, a flicker of light catches my eye up where the wall meets the drop ceiling. If I can climb up and push past the white ceiling panels, I could get above the water and maybe walk on beams in the ceiling. I frown. Or fall smack down on the concrete slab, break my bones and meet my death.

Gritting my teeth, I resolve to end this cruel game, one I never asked to join.

I cup my hands and call, "Is there anyone here?"

A rustling reaches my ears. I hope it's not a water snake. Although I was cavalier about the clown throwing one down on me, I'd rather not face that fear a second time today.

"Hey, is anyone there?"

With a screech, something metal moves in what might be the next room.

"Halloo? Hello? Hullo?"

I clear my throat. Water laps at my knees.

"I could use some help? Please? Help?"

Fingers grip a white ceiling panel and shift it over to the side.

A woman in her thirties with round rosy cheeks appears. Her brown hair is curly, and she's grinning.

I blow out a breath. "Am I glad to see you."

"All you had to do was ask for help," she says. "It's the magic word. Well, for you, it is. Not for me. Mine is more like give me more staff to get the job done. Or I don't want to work weekends again." She shrugs. "But whatever, right? At least it pays the bills, and I was able to buy my own private island. It's just a piece of rock jutting out of the Salish Sea, but it's all mine. Oh, sorry. I forgot to give this to you."

A thick rope drops from the ceiling.

It's two inches in diameter with knots in it for climbing.

Putting my hands together, I say, "Thank you so much. What a life saver."

"That's up to you. To save yourself, I mean. Think you can climb up?"

"Sure."

I wade through the stinking water that's up to my crotch over to the rope. I must be stronger than I've ever been. I don't want to die in bacteria-infested water. My mother would hate that. She's germ-phobic, and it would give her nightmares. I don't want to leave her like that.

I grasp a knot in the rope with both hands. "Here goes."

Her eyes grow wide. "It's your last shot, I hear. It's come on up or die time."

With a grunt, I pull myself up. My feet fly around before locating a knot to stand on. My armpits are damp with sweat.

When I look down, the cloudy water below is receding.

"Almost there," she says. "I'm Piper. And what's your magic word?"

"Help," I whisper, conserving my energy for climbing. I was never a fan of fitness classes or working out at the gym. But I do yoga and lift weights at home. Maybe it's paying off.

By the time I reach the top, I'm panting and out of breath. My thigh muscles are twitching. My biceps burn, and my hands are raw from handling the rope.

Piper offers a warm, firm, steadying hand and guides me to spot on a rafter beam.

"You okay to sit here and talk?" she says, plunking

down beside me. She hands me a red Chaos logo t-shirt. "Here, put this on."

I pull the t-shirt over my head. The fabric smells new and feels scratchy against my bare skin. Gripping the rafter beam, I let my legs dangle and half-smile to myself. I made it another step toward freedom.

"I'd rather be in a café having coffee," I say, "but this beats death by inhaling tainted water. What is this place?"

The wood-paneled attic feels like I stepped back in time. Over in a corner, they laid plywood for flooring over the rafters. A granny's rocker with flowered fabric cushions sits near a floor lamp decorated with dangling tassels. A small bookshelf is filled with books. With a sigh, I imagine sitting there instead of fighting for my life.

"It's on a need-to-know basis, and you don't have clearance," she says. "Now tell me about what happened at your camp when you were young. You've been avoiding that topic, and our surveillance indicates you've been doing that with friends and family. By filling out that survey, you gave us permission to view your email, texts, and phone conversations, although you rarely talk on those devices. I mean who wants to pick up the phone and talk to someone? I certainly don't."

I gape, dumbfounded by their monitoring my electronic communications. It's illegal and a violation of privacy. Not only is it wrong, but how much do these people know about me?

"I didn't agree to that."

She shrugs. "It was in the fine print on the privacy notice. I heard you skidded right past the pertinent language and checked the box that you'd read it and agreed to the terms."

I gulp and scold myself. Guilty as charged.

"On social media," she says, "you avoid engaging in conflict. I think that's the way we all should be in an ideal world, so I commend you for taking that stance. And if anyone mentions death or dying or fatal accidents, you shut your device down for hours."

A headache pulses in my temples. My fingernails dig into my palms.

"How do you know all this? What gives you and your company the nerve to pry into my personal business? It ticks me off, I can't tell you how much."

"Hey there," she pats the wooden rafter between us. "Don't freak out about it. You also gave consent when you filled out your Cabin Eight registration form. Remember? It had all that fine print? I watched the surveillance footage, and it looked like you skimmed right over what it said, and you again signed your rights away. Everything we know is because you invited us in to view the secret corners of your life."

Letting out a long, slow whistle, I shake my head. I should've been more careful. My mom warned me about reading the fine print and scams, but I thought that danger didn't apply to me, only to older, less savvy folks like her. This is my fault. I invited the monster into my house.

I might as well talk about the death at summer camp and get it out in the open. My mom has bugged me for years to see a therapist, but they're all booked, even the ones who only offer online counselling. What's the world coming to if you can't even get in to see a family counselor?

"What do you want to know?" I say in a quiet voice.

She nods. "That's a good first step. How about we go somewhere more comfortable to talk? It isn't easy on the butt, is it, sitting up here."

"It's not. But I refuse to go to a lab for tests. Whatever happens, you can't go all medical-testing on me and observe me like I'm in an experiment."

Piper stands. "I think we can accommodate your request."

18

Piper leads me down plywood steps into what looks like a cozy den in an upscale home. There's a fire going in a gas fireplace. I pad along on soft gray carpet and stand by the blazing fire, shivering and rubbing my arms to get warm.

Piper opens a closet and tosses me a plastic-wrapped package.

"Go put these on. There's a bathroom over there. You can shower too. You might feel better if you do. And don't try to leave. All exits are locked. We have 24/7 surveillance in all rooms."

As I trudge to the bathroom, she says, "Hey, don't be down about it. If you answer the questions honestly, we might let you go. If not, who knows what will happen?"

I scowl at her. "I'm not a guinea pig or some subject to be dissected."

She holds up her hands. "We're doing it for your good as well as for research purposes. Have you considered that?"

Shaking my head, I say, "Nope, that thought didn't occur to me. And I doubt it. I think you're all up to no good here and doing nefarious studies under the guise of a greater design for the common good."

"If you get out of here, we can meet over a beer and have a deeper discussion about that."

I say, "Or we could skip it. Once I leave here, I'm never coming near Two Rivers Resort again."

She shrugs. "Whatever, it's your call. If you make it out of here alive."

"Listen, I'm starving. Would you please bring me something to eat that's not tainted with sedatives or laced with a mysterious drug?"

"You bet. I was just about to do that."

I go in the bathroom and strip off my disgusting wet pants, leaving them on the floor in a corner. I never want to wear those again. Turning on the shower, I let hot water pound on my back until the tense muscles relax.

I take a bar of yellow Dial soap and shower off the filth. When I scrub at cuts on my hands to disinfect them, I wince with pain. I fill my mouth with water and wonder if it's possible to escape.

Was Piper telling the truth about letting me go after we talk, if I spill my guts? They could hold me forever in this underground facility. I have no way to communicate with the outside world.

Stepping out of the shower, I take my time drying off with a soft fluffy white towel. I'm in no hurry to spill my guts to a stranger and be vulnerable. Although Piper seems like a solid type of person, I now know I can't trust anyone.

I pull on a pair of gold-colored sweatpants and a matching hooded sweatshirt. They even gave me yellow socks to match. Each clothing item carries the Chaos corporate logo. I'm branded like a banana.

If I do manage to sneak out, others might think I'm an employee, so that's positive, and the sweatshirt hood will hide my face.

When I step out of the steamy bathroom, Piper is sitting by the fire. She's turned sideways with her short legs draped over the arms of an easy chair. She looks comfortable in her body, and I envy her confidence.

She says, "I brought you cream of asparagus soup and quinoa and kale salad."

She indicates a tray on a table by an armchair opposite her. A metal dome covers a plate.

Sniffing the air, the food doesn't smell bad. I'm not a fan of healthy foods, and I take a multi-vitamin to make up for it. I squint and stare at the tray. It smells like steak and potatoes with steamed broccoli, not what she described.

Sinking into a chair by the fire, I say, "I'm going to be honest. I hate the foods you listed. I'd rather eat steak and potatoes."

She smiles. "Just kidding. We read your profile. Lift the lid and see what you've got. You've worked hard, and you deserve a good meal before you open your heart and spit out your secrets."

Raising an eyebrow, I uncover the dinner plate. "I'll eat, but I'm not promising to tell you secrets. You're buttering me up, so I'll tell you the whole story, and you're going to be disappointed. It's not a big deal. Don't get high expectations, or you'll be bummed after I share."

"Eat up. I'll tell you a story about Chaos while you eat."

I shovel a bite of steak and garlic mashed potatoes into my mouth and lean back in the comfortable upholstered chair. My muscles relax with the fire's warmth. I almost groan, the food is so good. Then I drink a glass of water, eat more, and listen to her story.

"Twenty years ago, our founder Martin Truex discovered a better way to capture data and improve lives. He gathered the best minds he could find to explore his ideas and patent the research process. The result was this underground manufacturing facility with the best scientific laboratory in the country."

She pauses, sips her beer, and burps.

I open a can of Stella beer beside my plate and drink. Cold liquid slides down my throat like a whisper of good things to come. Oh, I hope this is the turning point, where all things bad change into something good. I could use a stroke of luck right about now.

"And?" I say, finishing my meal and digging into a piece of apple pie with crumble topping. The taste of tart and sweet explodes in my mouth.

"Do you have any ice cream to go with this?"

She shakes her head. "Nope, we're a dairy-free facility. Tough luck. Latex-free too, if you're thinking of sterile gloves."

Setting down my fork, I sit back and let out a contented sigh. At least my belly is full, and I'm warm. If only we could avoid talking about what happened when I was young.

To forestall the dreaded conversation, I say, "The food was good, especially the crumble on the pie. My mom used to make an apple brown betty with a topping like that. Is there a kitchen here, or do you order it from a restaurant?"

"We have a company cafeteria, where food is free for all employees."

My eyebrows lift. "Free?"

"Employees aren't allowed off campus during their week-long shifts. They sleep in plastic compartments with air vents that close. Like coffins, only bigger?" She wrinkles her nose like she doesn't approve of this and continues. "In addition to food being provided, we have special lights to emulate sunlight. Each person underground must sit in front of a happy light to read or work on their laptop for two hours each day. Otherwise, we've found workers get cranky without actual daylight."

Tilting my head, I say, "A week-long shift? That sounds awful. Who'd want to do that?"

Piper shrugs and finishes her beer, lifting the can upside down.

"They're paid well for the privilege of being employed in a top-notch facility. Some are drawn to the idea of doing ground-breaking research, and others by the money. Given the secret proprietary nature of our work, we don't always publish our results, which disappoints some scientists who want to share data with their peers. We make sure to patent every discovery twenty ways to Sunday. We've got a team of intellectual property lawyers grinding away, filing patent applications, but they're off site in Seattle."

Rubbing my lips, I realize the people behind this underground bunker have thought of everything. It's hopeless. I'll never be able to escape.

"Money isn't everything," I say. "I wouldn't agree to work here just for the cash."

"You're not like the people here, as I'm sure you know by now. That's why we recruited you for the study. Our team members believe in furthering science and pushing the boundaries, exploring concepts that haven't been focused on or advanced before. And now we're doing that. It's hard work but worth it." She beams with pride.

Crossing my legs, I say, "What about that spooky tall guy in the red robe in the labs? And the clown? You've got some freaky, frightening people here. Maybe you should look in their HR files and give them a personality test. You may have some psychopaths or narcissists or control freaks in your workforce."

She brushes off the comment with a wave of her hand. "We screen each person before they're hired, using a complex personality test to weed out the individuals with latent homicidal urges, and to alert us to those who might be difficult to work with. But when our research calls for a certain type of specialist, there might be only two or three individuals qualified in the world with the right experience and credentials. And we waive certain criteria."

I sit forward. "Take a closer look at whoever is playing the clown role. He's out of his gourd." When she casts her gaze on the fire, avoiding my eyes, I say, "Really, he's nuts. He's going to hurt someone."

She stands. "We're monitoring him, but it's no concern of yours. At least you managed to get past him and into my assigned area of the game. Let's go work out. We can talk about the topic you're avoiding while we're on treadmills."

My fingers dig into the arms of the chair. I was hoping not to approach that point in the conversation. "I just ate. It doesn't seem like the best time to exercise."

"Come on," she says. "It won't hurt you to go slowly on a treadmill while you talk."

I look around. "Won't people hear us? It's a private conversation. I don't want anyone other than you hearing what I might say."

"I reserved the gym. It'll be all ours. No excuses, let's go."

19

Entering the gym, I smell body odor and rubber yoga mats. A woman with a brown ponytail is running on a treadmill, feet thumping and hair bobbing with each step.

Piper goes over to her. "Clear the gym, remember? It's time."

The jogger pulls off her headphones. "What?"

"Clear out. I reserved it. For Subject One."

The runner pushes a button and stops the treadmill. She drapes her headphones around her neck and steps off, giving me a furtive glance.

My jaw drops. "Natalie? What are you doing here?"

When she starts to say something, Piper turns her by the shoulders and points to the door.

Piper says, "This is why I reserved the room. There

must be no interface with Subject One at this critical time. If she makes it out alive, talk to her then."

Natalie furrows her eyebrows and gives me a fleeting look before she hurries away.

Her surprised look makes me wonder if she wishes she wasn't working here. Or was she feeling guilty about not returning my texts? We'd been close in high school but lost touch when she was in college. Communication was hopeless when she was working on her doctorate and defending her thesis. I rack my brain, trying to recall what she studied, but I can't come up with it.

As Natalie walks out and the door closes, Piper says, "Now we can get started. Sorry about that. I know you used to know each other. That interaction just now never should've happened. Natalie's been acting odd lately and resisting adhering to our rules. You never know when it's time to let an employee go. Someone's an excellent worker and then wham, they're off the rails and have to be fired."

My eyes grow wide. "Last I heard, she loved her job. But I didn't know she worked here. She'd hate it if she was let go."

Piper turns her gaze to the bar bells. "Not everyone assimilates successfully into our system. One week on, one week off is difficult for some folks. They want to have a regular life and see friends, and to be able to talk about what they do at work. Which Chaos team members must never do. If they cross us and break that rule, we instantly have the right to deplete their bank accounts for the amount we've paid them during their employment with the company."

"What? Who would agree to that? I don't believe it."

"You'd be surprised by how many comply and authorize that in the event of a leak. We monitor their conversations at home as well as their personal phones for conversations and texts and emails containing confidential information. I shouldn't tell you this, but we house our former employees offsite at a detention center on a nearby island. That way, they can't leak confidential information."

"This is crazy," I say. "It's like something out of a dystopian thriller movie, where there's no escaping the all-knowing, all-powerful company who oversees your every move and knows every word you say. You probably have electronic transcripts of all your workers' conversations, don't you?"

She tilts her head and studies the ceiling.

I nod. "I'm right, aren't I? And why hasn't Chaos been taken to court for privacy violations?"

"Employees sign off and waive their rights," she says. "They want the money that much and are driven to make a difference. They want to be first in their field to make discoveries. We have the funding other companies lack. They can order all the expensive equipment they like. With a snap of the fingers, it's shipped out on the next truck. You name it, we'll buy it. Say for instance you want a Midmark M9D Autoclave? You don't have to write up a justification like at an academic research center or at one of our competitors. Just submit a request, and we'll go out and get it. We take care of our staff and go to great lengths to keep them happy."

I shake my head at how people have agreed to live curtailed lifestyles in order to have what appear to be unlimited budgets and access to the best equipment. If I were offered a bundle of money, would I sign away my rights? I might. Maybe I'm not that different from the people who work here. And it must be exciting to be on the cutting edge. Maybe that's why my friend Natalie took a job here. Now I understand why she couldn't tell me the name of the company that hired her, and she said it was hush-hush.

We don't have that in the house cleaning business. Well, unless you count the lace thongs tucked in a crack between sofa cushions. When you know the female of the house doesn't wear anything but granny panties. Or a bill marked overdue in red capital letters on a desk in the office, out in plain sight but not to be spoken of to others.

Piper clears her throat, bringing me back to the present. "And when a billionaire owns a start-up company, legal threats don't matter. They can do whatever they want if they have enough lawyers on the payroll to defend them and delay court cases and indictments."

Frowning, I say, "We're not all treated equally, are we, in the eyes of the law? It depends on how much money you have. It makes me furious."

She steps on a treadmill. "Come on sunshine, leave

your ignorance at the door and face facts. Money is in charge. Deep pockets can bend and shape the rules. The man who owns Chaos is Teflon in court. Nothing sticks to him."

I huff and throw up my hands. "I absolutely hate that about our system. What about the everyday working people like me? We're left in the dust, mowed down and plowed under by the power of a buck."

She says, "Don't go all Ayn Rand on me. Just get on a treadmill, and we'll talk."

I head to an exercise machine two over, leaving one between us, so she won't be able to hear me talk over the noise.

"Move over," she says, pointing to the treadmill next to her. "We've got to hear each other. I picked this activity for our discussion because research shows reserved people are more likely to open up and share if they're facing in the same direction. It makes it less threatening, not having eye contact, like sitting side by side in a car. It works best with teenage boys, I hear, if you want to get them to open up. Not that I'd know. I don't have kids."

She looks sad, so as I climb on the treadmill by hers, I say, "It must be impossible to have a family if you work here. Gone one week, back the next."

She nods. "Not so different than a firefighter's life."

She eyes me and I cringe, reminded of the fire I caused at the motel.

"Besides," she says, "most of our employees are in

their mid to late twenties or early thirties. They're hooked on work and want to fast track their research. They stay on campus to monitor their experiments even on their days off."

She chuckles. "We recruit in the summer, when the weather's great, we hire in the fall, and in the winter it's so gray and rainy here, they stay inside and work extra shifts for free. They're salaried positions with no over time."

"So, they're married to their jobs," I say, starting to walk on the treadmill.

"Pretty much. We just hire the driven ones. We weed out the liars and dishonest ones who would fib and fudge on data. We need solid repeatable research to lock in patents and keep out competitors."

It's a crazy world, this corporate stuff, and so foreign from my everyday job. I might as well be hearing about the details of launching astronauts into space. Still, I get it, the urgency to be first with a discovery and to lock in the rewards. But working in an office has never been a goal of mine.

I couldn't stare at a computer screen all day or work in a lab for hours. Someday, I hope to find a job that calls upon my need to organize messes and make living spaces shine with cleaning products. My mom is great, but I'd rather find my own path and work for myself.

Reminded of my mother, I recall how when I was a teenager, she'd take me for a drive. We'd sit in silence until I turned the radio on. Fifteen minutes later, she'd pull into Golden Gardens Park. We'd sit side by side staring at the water and looking west. Watching moody gray water, I'd start to talk about what was bothering me, and she'd listen. Usually it was about some injustice, a lower grade than I'd expected or my friends turning on me and gossiping.

The fact that my dad died when I was in middle school made me stand out as different. Other girls had fathers, even if they didn't live in the same house with them all the time. My dad never came home from kayaking that December day.

The Harbor Patrol issued an alert. The next day they found his blue kayak upside down, with his body inside. The current had carried him far from Blake Island. The kayak spray skirt was still in place. I guess he wasn't able to flip his boat right side up, and he drowned.

I shiver. What an awful way to die. Sucking in water when you want to live. Although you're desperately seeking air, you're trapped. Even if a rogue wave knocked you over, you'd know it was your fault. Because you were the one who decided to go kayaking solo instead of going to see the in-laws.

I don't think my mom's folks ever forgave him, even though he was dead, for not coming along that day to see them in La Conner. If he had, he'd still be alive, they said. But that was years ago, and they've passed away.

Walking slowly on the treadmill, I tell myself I'm pretty much over my dad's death, at least as much as is possible. But I do wish I'd been there with him and somehow saved his life. How awful it must be to be utterly helpless.

I think of the women in the big barn. They're trapped in there, like my dad was in his kayak. I must do something to help them.

I silently make a vow to stop Chaos Biotechnology. I'll find a way to free the women in the barn, no matter what it takes. If I can, I'll rescue Natalie, and I'll bring the place down. If ever a place needed to be brought to heel for inhumane treatment of human subjects, little green frogs, and former employees, this is it.

I clench my jaw, drawing a bright line in the sand and claiming this as my battle to win. I'm a nobody and lack executive powers and privileges, but I'll rain justice down on this company. I'm not a natural-born heroine, but someone needs to do it.

"Come on," she says. "Let's get going. Go a little faster. You're at a crawl."

Pushing a button, I select a slightly faster speed and plod along on the treadmill. I've had enough stress, surprises, and exertion in the hours I've been underground for a lifetime.

"Out of curiosity," I say, "where is the detention center for former employees? I've never heard of it."

"And you never will. That's how it's set up. Payments are made, and no one is the wiser. But if you must know, it's on Cedar Island. We don't want secrets leaking, given the sensitive nature of our work." She chuckles. "Once you're part of the Chaos family, you're with us forever. And don't tell your friend Natalie this, but she might end up there if she continues to violate our code of conduct."

Walking beside Piper, I bite my lip. Cedar Island is across the channel from Millersville, where Two Rivers Resort is located on the outskirts of town, well away from prying eyes. I can't let Natalie be taken there.

My stomach sinks as a thought occurs to me. Piper divulged the name of the island with the secret center housing former employees. I wonder if that means they intend to keep me here forever.

I grit my teeth. Subject One won't put up with imprisonment. They can't lock me in forever. But I need to concoct a plan and find my way out soon before it's too late. For all I know, they'll force me to talk about my secrets, draw my blood, drug me, and ship me off to a facility on an isolated island with no means of escape.

Striding briskly next to me, Pipe wipes her brow. "Now let's get to the topic you've been avoiding. You have thirty minutes to tell me about what happened, and your part in it. Otherwise, we're sending you to Cedar Island."

She glances at her smart watch. "Starting now. Your choice. Tell or go."

My stomach sours. "I've got to go to the bathroom."

I shut down the treadmill and step off.

She says, "Like I said, you decide what happens next. Participate in our free discussion or clamp down and join others in the detention center. If that happens, we'll close the file for Subject One and mark it as a failed experiment." She taps her wrist. "You've already wasted two minutes. What do you want to do?"

I step on the treadmill and turn it on. "Fine, but I don't see what this has to do with an experiment."

"Martin Truex came up with the idea. Like I said before, we have a hypothesis. We're testing an idea about the impact of trauma when young on world views and outcomes as adults. You'll be helping other subjects. We'll refine our theory based on what you say and adjust later tests that we'll conduct."

I say, "I'm not doing any tests. I'm not a lab rat."

"It's a lie detector test, nothing invasive. Remember, you're helping us gather data to assist others in the future."

"Fine," I say. "Let's get this over with."

20

I stare at a blank wall in front of me and consider how to start discussing my friend's death. Casting my gaze around the room to buy a bit more time, my eyes snag on a bright colored poster. "Watch what you say here and everywhere. We're listening. Don't make us come for you. You'll regret it." The laughing cartoon face with a lolling tongue looks out of place with the threatening words.

Drawing in a deep breath, I dive in and talk. I know I need to heal from what happened, and this exercise might help me get over the trauma. Nothing else has worked.

"Fine," I say, "here's what happened. When I was twelve, I was summer camp for the second time. I was happy there. We were in the middle of nowhere with a river going by and a big meadow where we'd camp. My cabin and another one went off on a canoe trip for three days."

My hands are clammy, and I wipe them on my sweatpants.

Piper is quiet. She walks beside me and stares straight ahead, as if a spot on the wall is fascinating and holding her attention.

"We paddled hard and camped along the river."

I cough and clear my throat. Come on, I tell myself. Spit the story out and get this over with. Maybe you'll feel better afterwards.

"On the second day, I don't know how it happened, but Fiona drowned. One minute we were standing in the river, water rushing past us, and then she took a few steps into deeper water.

She said, "Look at me, I'm a mermaid. I'm a champion swimmer."

She grinned at me, did a few breaststrokes and then she was carried away by the current."

"And?" Piper probes.

"The next time I saw her she was dead. What gets me most is I can still see her swimming, hair fanning out, with a big grin on her face. I tried to grab her arm to pull her back in. But she was long gone, and the river was too strong. She was jerked away before I could save her."

I clutch my chest and sob. Tears run down my cheeks. I've kept this inside for too many years and carried guilt about not saving her. Whenever I hear a loud noise or someone screams, I flinch and the image of Fiona disappearing in the rushing water flashes before my eyes.

My secret has been a festering boil. It's time to slice it open.

"All I remember is hearing screams. Two camp counsellors were shouting and running down a path by the river. I followed them, and we searched for an hour."

"What did you find?"

"I didn't. It was Libby, a counsellor, who did. She came out of the river carrying Fiona in her arms. She was weeping as she laid her body down on the muddy beach. Mona, another camp counsellor, gave her mouth to mouth and pounded on Fionna's chest, but Fi didn't move on her own.

"When Mona gave up and said there was no hope, I fell to my knees and did mouth to mouth and CPR for the longest time. It was awful, seeing Fiona limp and lifeless like that and touching her cold lips. I was crying. I sat back to catch my breath."

Mona patted my back and told me to stop.

"In a soft voice, she said, 'She's dead. We've got to tell the others and get back to camp.'"

Piper looks at me with wide eyes. "Didn't they call 911 for help?"

"We were in the middle of nowhere, and Libby was an EMT. She'd done all she could. I'm not even sure if the counsellors had phones or a cell signal. It was that remote."

In a wavering voice, I say, "It was an accident, but I've felt guilty about it ever since. Why didn't I grab her? I could've saved her."

I shudder. "You can't imagine what she looked like. That was not my friend Fi, but a horrible replacement. She appears in my nightmares. We wrapped her body in a sleeping bag and placed her in a canoe. The counsellors said they could do it without me, but I insisted on helping. She was my best friend and bunk mate, after all. She'd have wanted me to help and be gentle with what remained. I took the spot in the canoe in front of Fi and paddled in the bow while Mona the counsellor steered from the stern. Our group was dead silent as we paddled back to camp."

In a choked voice, I manage to say, "We paddled into camp, and instead of our usual tap, tap, tap, salute with our paddles, we remained silent and glided ahead, out of respect for the dead. We were silent, as tears streaked down our cheeks."

With a gasp, I run over to a waste basket and vomit, spewing out steak, pie, and potatoes.

I fall to my knees and wail.

This is why I didn't want to talk about the awful incident.

I say, "Fiona, I'm sorry, I should've saved you. It's my fault you died."

Piper turns to a large mirror on the wall. "You getting this?"

Wiping spittle from my mouth, I stare at her. "What are you talking about?"

She doesn't answer and looks at the low-pile industrial carpet.

Pointing, I say, "Is that a one-way mirror?"

She shrugs. "Sure, it is. We're recording the session, so we can study it later."

I stand and put my hands on my hips. "The hell you are."

Running over, I grab two ten-pound bar bells and heave them at the mirror.

Glass cracks. Shards fly past.

I yell, "That's it. I've had enough. You won't be watching me anymore."

The mirror collapses and falls to the floor, revealing Mr. Red Robe and Ms. Goggles. Their mouths hang open.

He picks fragments of glass off his cape and glares at me.

"Martin Truex, I presume?" I say. "The brains behind the operation?"

His face is lean like a long-distance runner. His blue eyes are small and close together. Dark smudges under his eyes make him look as worn and haggard as I feel.

"We weren't supposed to meet like this," he says. "And I didn't want you to know my name. But now, I suppose, it's too late to reverse this unfortunate event. You've infiltrated our group and gleaned secrets, eliciting them one by one. You're far cleverer than we anticipated."

I grimace, thinking of how I intend to expose his company. He hasn't seen anything yet. I'll show him what clever looks like. The trouble is, I don't have a specific plan, so I'll have to wing it.

He turns to Piper, who is standing by my side. Her jaw is tense. She's shoved her hands into her pockets.

"And you," Martin Truex booms, pointing at Piper, who is shaking. "You divulged the location of our corporate retreat center. No one outside the company has ever spoken about it with outsiders or given the location."

To distract him from the fact that I have that important information and to protect Piper, who has been kind to me, I say, "Listen Mr. Red Robe, she was using it as a tool to gain my trust. If she hadn't given me that bit of information, I wouldn't have participated in your project and talked about my past. I've already forgotten the location she mentioned. Was it in a desert somewhere? Or Alaska?"

"We can always give you a polygraph test," he says. "Better yet, a truth serum."

Ms. Goggles says, "Sorry, sir, but we ran out of truth serum last week. It's on back order."

He barks, "Who is responsible for that? I want them fired this instant and thrown off the premises."

She shrugs. "It's no one's fault. Supply chain issues, I heard. Out of our hands. Beverly said she put in the requisition when our supplies were low."

Putting a hand to his forehead, he says, "Damn it, how

are we going to conduct research and test our theories without that?"

"Piper did a good job," I say. "Without giving me drugs to make me talk, she made feel comfortable. You might try a nicer approach, instead of being Mr. Nasty Pants as a boss."

The corners of Ms. Goggles's mouth turn up, and she gives a slight nod.

Piper says, "She's got a good point."

He claps his hands. "That's enough. We'll discuss it in the Steering Committee and see where the responsibility lies for the system failure."

Shaking his head, he says, "No truth serum. How will we proceed with our experiments on human subjects without that? It's in our protocol. We can't vary our standard operating procedures at this point."

This guy is crazy. He's so close to chasing his cause that he's lost sight of what's right and wrong. I hope the lack of truth serum seriously screws up their research.

I smile because this new development will definitely help me. I didn't want to get stung by a needle and spew out secrets. Now I can skip that part of their diabolical plan.

I decide to change the subject and put in a good word for Piper because she's been kind to me, for the most part. She fed me and got me out of the sewage-filled room by tossing down the rope.

"Piper is excellent at her job," I say, "and she deserves a raise."

She gives me a smile. "How about it, boss?"

He frowns and strokes his chin, where there's a five o'clock shadow.

Pulling up his hood and obscuring his face, he ignores my suggestion and says, "We'll have to take more serious measures now to make sure you comply with our requests."

Chaos isn't going to mess with my mind. I'm not a guinea pig or a test subject.

"I gave you the information you wanted," I say. "I think you're cruel. You enjoy torturing people and tiny green frogs."

"Lock her up," he says. "She's spouting nonsense. She needs to be sedated."

Tensing my muscles, I get ready to run. I shout, "No way."

As I scramble ahead, Martin Truex yells, "After her."

Bursting through the door into a hallway, I shove a heavy bookcase against the door.

The smell of split pea soup and fresh-baked bread wafts past.

I glance across the hall into the cafeteria.

Fifty people in white lab coats are sitting at tables. They turn my way and gape. A woman with short hair and yellow-rimmed glasses points at me.

"That's Subject One. Something must have gone wrong. She's out there alone."

"No one's with her," a man says.

My heart pounds. My body breaks out in a cold sweat. I jerk my head around, searching for an escape.

Down the hall is a door with an exit sign above it.

I pump my legs and race ahead.

I'm running, running, running for my life.

I have no idea where I'm going, but it doesn't matter.

I've got to get out of the clutches of Chaos Corporation.

When I slam my hips against the door and push on the bar, it flies open.

21

I'm standing outside the building in the pouring rain. I sniff the air. It smells like damp pine needles. The odor of split pea soup spews out from a nearby exhaust vent.

Across a well-lit blacktop parking lot is a tall chain link fence with barbed wire on top running around the perimeter. My heart ticks. I drum my fingers on my crossed arms as I mull over what to do next.

I've got to get out of here, but I don't see a way forward except running for it. The way the company is run with airtight processes and many loyal employees, I doubt I'd get far on foot. I glance back at the exit door. I've only got a few seconds left to make a choice.

A delivery truck pulls in and parks. A painted sign on the side shows colorful vegetables with the words

"Sandy's Produce." The driver hops out and goes to the back.

I skitter over and hide behind a bush to get a better look and plan my escape.

She rolls up the back of the truck.

While she stacks cardboard boxes on a hand truck, I crouch down and creep over to her cab, slipping inside. The truck smells like roses. In a small vase glued to the dashboard is a pink rose.

She left the key in the ignition, perhaps because this is a secure facility in the middle of nowhere.

I hunker down, so she won't notice me, and surveillance cameras won't pick up my location. It's tough to remain hidden in a yellow sweat suit. Grimacing, I hope I didn't swallow some weird geo-tracking solution with my food or beer. I won't underestimate what Chaos can do.

She wheels her cart to the door I came through and hits a button by the door.

"Delivery."

A buzzer sounds, and she opens the door, wheeling the boxes inside.

I turn the key and start the truck.

I lock the doors and slam my foot on the accelerator.

I'm getting the heck out of here.

Just then, Ms. Goggles, Martin Truex in his red robe, and Piper run out. They're waving their arms and shouting. People in white lab coats come outside and stand on the sidewalk, blocking Mr. Red Robe and the others from coming after me.

Someone pounds on the side of the truck. Martin Truex tries to open the passenger door, and he bangs on the window. He's red in the face and his hood has fallen off. He looks like a normal person now.

I give him the finger and floor it, leaving him in the dust.

Coming to a guard shack, I blow through a chain link fenced gate.

Fencing slams into the windshield and drapes over the truck engine. I drive on, metal scraping as I rumble down the road. People are in trouble, and I've got to save them. I'll pay for the gate and return the truck later. Right now, lives are at stake.

I head in the direction of the big barn with the captive women inside. From what I saw on the monitor in the lab, it might be on the same road as the barn I entered.

I fly by the barn I was locked in. The truck engine whines. When I hit a series of potholes and bounce out of them, my teeth chatter. The small of my back is tight with tension.

When I pull up to a large rundown barn, I turn the truck off and shove the key in my pocket. I jump down on the ground and scope out the area. I don't see any Chaos employees. Not yet, anyway.

I raise my fist to the dark night sky. My muscles are

thrumming with pent up energy. I'm invincible. I'll release the women and set them free at any cost.

Although I couldn't save my friend at camp, I'll rescue these women and protect them from harm and certain death.

I flinch as a woman screams.

It sounds like she's running toward me and approaching fast.

She yells, "There she is. Get her."

"Stop her," another says.

A gold disc whizzes past my head as I run to the barn door.

My arms are pumping, and my heart is racing.

I throw the board aside that locked it and slide open the door.

Women crowd around me. "Help us!"

I point to the Sandy's Produce truck.

"I'm here to help. We don't have time to talk. Stay low and run to the truck and get in. Don't let the frisbees hit you."

Wham.

A gold disc slams into the barn, right by my head.

Splinters of wood fall to the ground.

I pick up the disc and cock my arm. It's heavy and has sharp metal edges. This is a lethal weapon.

"Climb in the truck while I hold them back. Don't worry. We'll get out of this."

Another frisbee whizzes into the barn, barely missing our heads.

A middle-aged woman with curly hair bends down and picks it up.

She says to me, "Nice to meet you." To the others, she says, "Run to the truck. We'll distract them. It's time to get even."

The other prisoners fly to the truck and climb in.

Gold frisbees zing by, whistling past my ears.

Ms. Curly and I throw discs at our enemies and run to the truck, hopping in.

I lock the doors, turn the key and step on the accelerator.

Gold discs hit the truck and smack into the windshield, cracking it.

A line of women dressed in black appears in front of us, blocking the dirt road.

The disc throwers are members of the company's elite trained force. They cross their arms and stare into the headlights. They look grim and fierce with tight mouths.

The shortest one steps forward and holds up a hand.

"Hold it right there. We've changed our minds. We're with you, not against you."

Rolling down the window, I say, "I don't believe you. Move aside, and we'll pass. If you don't, I'll have to run you down to save these women."

"They locked us in," a woman beside me in the passenger seat says. "Don't trust them."

I say, "Don't worry, I won't."

"Come out and talk with us," the short leader says. "We've had a change of heart."

"That's bullshit," I say. "You're afraid justice is about to knock on your door. Move or I'll be forced to gun it. These women need medical care."

The leader says, "It's not our fault. We were just following orders."

I clear my throat. We'd better get on the move or more of Chaos's employees will appear and swarm the truck, incapacitating us.

I say, "Step aside. This is your final warning. If you help us and make sure the others don't come after us, the authorities will go easier on you, I bet."

"Fall back," she says to the line of disc throwers. "Let them pass and do all you can to prevent people from pursuing them."

The disc throwers run off and disappear into the darkness.

I slam on the accelerator, and the truck roars ahead.

The group in the truck cheer and clap and break into laughter.

"We're free," one says.

"Finally," another yells.

I think about calling the police, but I don't have a phone. And I suspect the police are in cahoots with Chaos. Local officials could be bribed to look the other way. All it would take is one lone patrol officer on the take to give the company an unfair advantage tonight.

Just in case, I say, “Anyone have a phone?”

“No, they took our things,” the woman next to me says.

“Look in the glovebox. Maybe there’s something we can use in there.”

A police car pulls up and blocks the road.

“I suspect the police are in on this,” I say. “We’re lost. There’s no hope.”

The women groan.

The woman in the passenger seat says in an upbeat voice, “I found something.”

She pulls a cell phone from the glove compartment and pushes a few buttons. “We can use it. It’s not locked. No access code required.”

I say, “But who can we call? We can’t go to the police.”

Then I remember Ned, the reporter in Seattle. She’d help us and uncover the story. She’d rip the lid off this secret operation. I bet she’d help me find and free the fired employees who are being held on Cedar Island.

“I’ve got an idea that just might work.”

I take the phone and dial the reporter’s cell. She’s called so often that I’ve memorized her number.

When Ned answers, I say, “It’s Miranda. I need your help. There’s trouble in Millersville. A covert Chaos Biotechnology facility is trapping people and using them for experiments. I just escaped and freed prisoners from a barn, but the police are stopping us from leaving.”

A police officer gets out of a patrol car.

Speaking into a megaphone, he says, "Get out of the truck with your hands up."

My hand trembles as I say into the phone, "Did you hear that? They want us to surrender. They'll lock us up again. You wouldn't believe what they did to us."

"Miranda, don't get out of the truck. Tell the officer I want to talk to them. Get a badge number. If they're paid to go along with this, it might be one rogue officer and not the whole force. Can you make out the license plate of the cop car?"

Squinting to see better, I give her the license plate number.

"Okay, I'm on it. You say it's Chaos Biotechnology running the operation?"

"Yes, and Martin Truex is the one in charge. It's his company. I think they have a contract with the Department of Defense and are manufacturing a secret compound for military use. Oh, here comes the police officer."

"Put me on speaker and hold the phone out the window, but don't give it to him, or let him take it from you."

"Got it."

Using a bright flashlight, a stocky police officer peers into the truck.

"Roll down your window," he says.

When I do that, he says, "I told you to exit the vehicle. Get out and keep your hands above your heads."

"We're not doing that," I say. "A Seattle reporter knows about the situation here, and she wants to speak to you. I told her I suspect you may be taking bribes from Chaos Biotechnology."

He rubs his upper lip and mumbles something under his breath.

I put the phone on speaker and hold it up to the window.

"Hello Officer, my name is Ned Bagley, and I'm a reporter for The Stranger in Seattle. Who am I speaking with?"

"Officer Cahorn from the Millersville Police. Why are you nosing around? There isn't a story here. No need to investigate normal business operations."

"I'll determine that after I look into it. What's your badge number, Officer Cahorn?"

He mumbles the badge number and adds, "I don't need this hassle. They told me it'd be easy extra work on the side. Just a bunch of women being kept in a barn. No big deal."

He spits on the road.

Ned says, "I didn't get your badge number. Could you repeat it, louder this time?"

When he gives it in a louder voice, Ned says, "Officer, I suggest you disengage from the situation and think long and hard about stopping these women from leaving. From what I understand, they've done nothing wrong. Chaos Biotechnology could be charged with capturing hostages, holding humans in captivity, and subjecting them to experiments."

The officer coughs. "I'll give it some thought."

"Will you let them go? I suggest you do that."

He shrugs. "Sure, why not?"

To me, he says, "I'll deal with Mr. Truex. You can drive ahead. You're free to go."

I accelerate, and the women cheer as the truck leaps ahead.

Steering around the police car, I wonder what's ahead.

I say to Ned, who is still on the line, "I'm not sure what to do now. We made it out alive, but we have nowhere to go. We need water, food, blankets, and a safe shelter."

Ned says, "Come back to Seattle and bring the women you freed. I don't think we can trust the police or bring them in on this yet. I have some research to do first."

"I stole a Sandy's Produce delivery truck. I have to return it. It's pretty beat up from what we went through, but I'll pay for repairs."

"I'll arrange for a van to pick you up. Leave the truck, and I'll tell the produce company where it is. Just get back to town. I want to interview all of you while it's fresh in your minds. This'll make a great story as long as we can get you back to the city alive."

"How will I know it's your driver in the van, and not someone from Chaos come to force us to go back?"

"I'll send my brother. He's got a white unmarked van with space for you all. He's got a long, scraggly beard, and he'll be wearing a yellow ball cap."

"What's his name, and where will we meet?"

"Meet him at the I-5 North rest stop near Marysville. It's got a huge hollowed out tree you can walk through. His nickname is Frodo, and your password is Foxy Lady."

Gripping the steering wheel tight as I drive toward I-5, I snort. "That's a terrible password. Can't you think of a better one? Like Underground Caves?"

"It'll work," she says. "I'll text my brother now."

A car comes up behind us, about a mile back. I turn off on a private drive, kill the engine and douse the headlights. The engine ticks.

I say in a hushed voice, "Everyone be quiet."

"What's going on there?" Ned says by phone.

A sedan whooshes past without slowing or stopping.

In the truck, we all release loud breaths.

I start the engine and turn back on the two-lane deserted road.

"Just a car on the road," I say. "I'm being cautious. We'll see Frodo in about half an hour, I hope."

22

Pulling into a rest stop off I-5 near Marysville, I park near the restrooms and a huge hollowed out tree. The women want to hit the restrooms and check out the tree, but I shut that down before it gets out of hand.

"We're sitting ducks here in a Sandy's Produce truck. They know I stole it, and they'll be looking for us. We need to stay together until the reporter's brother shows up."

A knock on the driver's side door makes me squeal.

A man with a long, straggly beard and a yellow ball cap is standing there.

"Let's go," he says, pointing to a white unmarked van.

His eyes are cold and flat. When he steps closer, his beard looks fake. I can make out elastic bands around his ears holding it in place.

He says, "I'm Ned's brother. Come with me. It's safe."

Another white van pulls into the lot and parks next to us.

The woman in the passenger seat next to me whispers, "Ask him the password."

"What's the password?" I say to him, keeping the doors locked.

He glares. "Underground Caves. Come on, we're in a hurry."

"I don't think so," I say.

I honk the horn, and people look over.

A man with a long beard and a yellow ball cap hurries over from a white van. "Is this man bothering you? I'm Ned's brother, and she sent me to pick you up."

I bite my lip. What if Chaos sent more than one man to impersonate Ned's brother and confuse me? My mind races ahead, imagining the worst outcome. What if we climb in the wrong van, the doors lock, and we're held as prisoners? I shudder. Anything but that fate.

I study the two men. Either one could be Ned's brother, but my hunch is the first man with cold eyes and what looks like a fake beard is an imposter from Chaos. I've got to go with my gut.

I say to the man with a false beard, "You're not Ned's brother. Go on, get out of here. You're not fooling us."

The other man, who I hope is Ned's relative, says, "That's right, beat it."

The fake brother runs back to his van and peels

rubber as he floors it, swerving around a pair of gray-haired senior citizens making their way to a Sprinter RV. Last I saw him, he was on his phone while driving.

My stomach tightens, picturing Chaos ramping up operations to chase us. Please, don't come after us. I hope my friend Natalie left or she'll be shipped off to Cedar Island.

Rolling my window down, I say to the bearded fellow, "What's the password?"

"Foxy Lady," he says with a grin. "What a cheesy choice. Ned's much better at investigating and writing stories than coming up with secret passwords. Although yours was good. Underground Caves was creative. Let's go before the cops show up."

I hope my instincts are right, and this is Ned's brother. If not, we'll be dragged back to the underground labs and subjected to experiments.

"The chase is on. Let's go," I say, unlocking the doors and wiping down surfaces to remove fingerprints. To the women, I say, "This is Ned's brother Frodo, and he's going to drive us."

As we pile out, a woman says, "I have to go to the bathroom."

"We don't have time," I say, "they're coming for us."

Frodo says, "I've got a bucket you can use."

"That's disgusting."

I hide the truck keys in the wheel well and join the others in the van, hopping into the front passenger seat.

"Okay," I say, "Floor it."

A woman says, "Wait, wait, we left someone behind."

Turning around, I see a woman running after us and waving her hands. What if she's a plant from Chaos and wasn't really with us? I'm not sure if I've seen her before.

To be truthful, the woman who spoke up seems new too. Did they manage to infiltrate our small group already? They could've come along with the fake brother and slipped in with our group when we got out of the truck.

When Frodo brakes and comes to a stop, I touch his arm.

"Hold on, we may have spies. I'm not sure I've seen that woman's face before."

"Me neither," says a woman with dark circles under her eyes.

We probably all look like that, after what we've been through.

"Who are you talking about?" a thin woman says. "The woman running or the one in the van who just spoke up?"

"Both," we all say at once.

The woman who asked us to stop scowls. "I was with you all along. We were stuck together."

"Lock the doors," I whisper to Frodo, "just in case."

I say to her, "Where were you all stuck together? Describe the place."

She looks confused. She tugs on a strand of black hair and puts it in her mouth, chewing on it. "Why are you asking? You know the answer. I was there with you all, wasn't I?"

Only a liar wouldn't answer the question. I decide to test her. "What color was the paint inside the cabin where you were staying?"

Her eyebrows arch. "The cabin? Hmm, I think they were yellow. Pale yellow?"

"Out," I say, "you weren't with us, and you're not a good fibber. Tell your boss you tried but failed. We outsmarted you and your friend. Everyone, don't talk to this woman or tell her anything."

To Frodo, I say, "Drive off and we'll let her out farther down the road. We've got to get going or they'll catch up with us."

When he steps on the gas, we zip out of the parking lot and merge onto the freeway.

"Hey," the infiltrator says, pounding on a window. "We need to go back for the other person. We can't leave her stranded."

"Oh, yes, we can," I say. "And you're next."

Five miles later, I say in a low voice to Frodo, "Pull over on the side of the freeway. We'll let her out here."

To the group in the back, I say, "We're making a quick stop to drop someone off. Make sure you don't get out, or you'll be left behind. Search the area around her for any tracking devices."

We stop on the shoulder of the freeway and, as cars whiz past, we open the van door. Frodo and I grab the agitator with black hair and yank her out. She squirms and kicks and tries to get back in the van with the others, but they block her way.

She says, "Chaos is the best thing that's happened to me. I've never been paid so well. I hope you fail."

"Good luck getting back," I say, climbing into the van and slamming the door shut.

As we merge onto the freeway, Frodo says, "Slick move back there, detecting a spy in our midst. Anyone find a microphone or tracking device tucked into the seat or on the floor?"

"Got one," a curly-headed disc throwing woman says, holding it up and grinning.

"If you give it to me," I say, "I'll throw it out the window."

I fling the bug out the window and hope it won't be long before we reach Ned's apartment in North Seattle. Only thirty miles to go.

A woman laughs, and it's contagious. We all chuckle.

I throw up my hands. "We're free!"

Voices chime in.

"I never thought we'd get out of the barn."

"Thank you for rescuing us."

I say, "I couldn't have done it without the reporter we're going to meet and Frodo."

"Why is she called Ned?" the woman with curly hair says.

"I don't know," I say. "Why is that Frodo?"

He smiles as he drives. "Our family assigned nick-names. She was called Ned because as a baby she looked like our Uncle Ned, and the name stuck."

He brakes as traffic slows on the freeway.

A vehicle rear ends our van, pitching us forward in our seats.

My seat belt locks, stopping me before I smack into the dashboard.

I say, "Everyone okay?"

"I bumped my head. Otherwise, I'm fine."

Frodo looks in the rear-view mirror and frowns.

"They're coming for us again. Brace for impact. I'll get us out of here."

He swerves onto the shoulder and drives past cars stuck in a traffic jam.

He races for the next exit. Horns blare. Fists shake at us as we fly past.

My pulse races. I hope Ned's brother can get us to safety.

I take a moment to look back.

Behind us, a pickup truck is coming up fast.

23

We're driving along the shoulder of the freeway, and I crane my neck for a better look at the truck following us. Wearing his red robe, Martin Truex is behind the wheel of a silver Ford F-250. He has a crazed look on his face. His rig has a grille guard like on a cop car, and it looks sturdy, like it could bash into the van for a long time and come out fine.

"He won't give up," I say to Ned's brother Frodo. "He's a maniac."

Frodo clenches his jaw. "No way I'll let him win. Ned's depending on me for transport to her place. I promised I'd deliver you there and protect you."

Ahead of us, a car is parked on the shoulder.

He slams on the brakes and comes to a stop before hitting it.

"I knew this was a dangerous assignment when I

agreed to it," he says. "Ned never does things the easy way. She pokes her nose in and stirs up trouble. She looks under the rug for dirt, she says, because she knows it's there."

He rolls down his window and waves a hand, nudging into traffic in the right lane.

We're crawling along at ten miles an hour.

Will we ever get to the reporter's apartment?

"How much farther?" I say, squirming in my seat.

"About five miles to the exit for her place. I think we lost him back there."

A white van pulls alongside and paces us in the middle lane.

The driver is the guy from the rest stop, still wearing a yellow ball cap. In his van is a woman who pretended to be part of our group. He motions to us to open the window.

She yells from the passenger seat, "Pull over. We want to talk with you."

"This is bullshit," Frodo says.

He punches the gas and veers off on an exit marked Transit Vehicles Only.

We come to a parking lot filled with buses.

A driver climbs out of a bus and wipes his brow. He looks tired. Maybe it's the end of his shift.

Frodo pulls up next to him.

"Hey, buddy, I've got to transport these women two miles away to my sister's place. Can you do me a favor?"

In a deep voice, the man says, "Depends." He hitches up his belt. "What's wrong? You look like you're in a hurry."

"I am, I promised I'd keep these women safe. But a crazy guy in a red robe is trying to take them back to his locked compound in a rural area up north."

"That's not right." The man steps closer to our van. "Did you call the police?"

I say, "We're going to as soon as we're safe."

He looks around and then says, "What'd need me to do?"

"Do you have a vehicle you can use to transport eleven women a few miles? They need to be dropped off at my sister's apartment by Bitter Lake."

He glances back at a shed, where a man is standing with a clipboard, watching us.

"I came in from my shift a few minutes early, so I might be able to help you. Hold on." He pulls out a handheld radio. "Requesting putting Number 384 back in service for a ten-minute mercy mission to transport a group of women who are in harm's way. I'll be back before you know it, boss. Just running over to Bitter Lake and back."

He clicks off and waits for a response.

I cross my fingers, hoping he'll get approval.

He says to Frodo and me, "I've got the best record on the crew. We'll see what he says. I wouldn't bet on it. He's got a tick in his side most days, but he was in a good mood this morning."

"Roger that, Ernie. You're cleared to go. Mark her as Out of Service and get back here before the others pull in. Don't tell anyone about this. I'm making an exception for you because I trust you and appreciate your work ethic."

"Thank you, sir."

He turns to us. "He's my father-in-law, so it greases the wheels sometimes. Get on the bus, and we'll get going."

Frodo says to me, "I'll divert them, in case they follow the van. Go to the corner of 130th and Greenwood. I'll meet you and take you to Ned's apartment."

We jump out of the van and run to Ernie's green and yellow Metro bus.

I sink into a seat behind the driver and blow out a deep breath. We made it this far. Only a little farther to go to get to Ned's place. With a frown, I wish I'd gotten her address and apartment number in case Frodo doesn't show up.

Someone in the back of the bus breaks into an impromptu song, and we all join in, celebrating our win. We're on our way. Soon Ned will take care of us. We're almost safe.

"Thanks, Ernie," I say from my spot behind the driver.

He grins at me in the rear-view mirror.

"Glad to help. Care to tell me what this is about? How did you end up needing transport on a bus?"

"It's a long story, and I hope you'll read about it in the

papers in the next few days. It's about corporate greed, a hidden underground manufacturing facility, clinical tests on unwilling human subjects, and a secret government contract."

He nods. "I look forward to reading it."

My eyebrows lift, and I nod back. I hope Ned will follow through and investigate, and her article will appear on the front page. I want Martin Truex and his company to be exposed, so no one else will experience what Chaos subjected us to.

We pass a small lake with benches, a grassy park, and a playground.

"That's Bitter Lake on our right," Ernie says. "We're approaching your destination. Prepare to disembark."

He stops the bus at the corner of 130th and Greenwood Avenue.

The doors open with a whoosh.

Ernie says, "This is where he said he'd meet you. It's been a pleasure driving you, and I wish you all the best."

"Thanks," I say, going down the steps.

We gather on the sidewalk. As Ernie drives off, we look around. There's no sign of Frodo's white van.

A white van comes around the corner fast and sideswipes a blue car.

I cringe, hearing metal scraping, and hope Frodo is about to join us.

Is Frodo in the van or will it be a Chaos employee? I'll know in a moment.

When the Chaos guy hops out of a vehicle, I say in a shaky voice to the others, "Come on, let's head to the apartments. We'll find the reporter."

The Chaos man tries to follow us, but the driver of the car he hit grabs his wrist and holds on. "You hit my car. You can't run from the scene of an accident. It's a crime."

As we run through a gate leading to the apartments, a woman in her late twenties appears and waves to us. Her blond-streaked hair is pulled back in a ponytail.

"I'm Ned Bagley, and I work for The Stranger," she says. "Frodo was held up. He's acting as a decoy for the silver pickup. Come right this way and move fast before they catch us."

She buzzes us into the building, and we pile into an elevator. With so many of us in a small space, we're pressed against each other's bodies. A rank smell of body odor fills my nose, and I breathe through my mouth. We could all use a shower.

I grin at Ned. "I'm glad you came out and found us."

"We're not out of danger yet. We've got work to do before we cross the finish line. Nice to meet you all." Ned smiles. "With your help, we'll turn the situation around and catch them at their game."

"Count me in," I say, and the others chime in.

"Yeah, I'll help."

"Me too."

"Let's get them back for what they did to us."

24

We gather in Ned's kitchen and dining area. We drink cups of coffee, gulp glasses of water, and wolf down bagels spread with cream cheese, crowding together. After what we've been through, being jammed together is comforting, as if the bones of the women conversing near me will cradle me through adversity.

I wait for a turn in the bathroom and rub my forehead, where a headache throbs.

A woman exits the bathroom and says to me, "I'd love to get in the shower and stand there for hours."

"Believe me," I say, "I feel the same way. I want to wash off what happened and let water pound on my back."

I close the door, do my business, and wash my hands. Looking in the mirror, I see a worn-out husk of a shell. Dark circles under my eyes tell me I've been somewhere I never want to go again. We must stop Chaos in its tracks before others are hurt and taken advantage of.

I've aged years in a few days, and I'm not finished. I want to rescue the former employees on Cedar Island. As soon as we tell our stories to Ned for her article, I'll be off to get that done and set them free.

I didn't set out to be a crusader for justice. I went to Cabin Eight to focus on myself. But the grueling tests underground formed me into a fierce advocate for others with a fire in my belly.

When I come out of the bathroom, the middle-aged woman with curly hair who helped me fend off security by throwing metal-edged discs introduces herself. "I'm Shawna." She gives me a hug, "Thank you for rescuing us. I don't know what we'd have done if you hadn't come along. We tried everything but couldn't get out of the barn."

I scuff my shoe on the carpet. "Someone had to do it. You were trapped. They were about to conduct experiments on you."

She slurps her coffee and sets the cup down on a coffee table in the living room. "What did they do to you?"

"A bunch of tests designed to test my stamina and see if they could drive me crazy. I had to crawl through an air duct. Later I escaped from a bare cement room that was flooding with stinking water. There was more. What I described was toward the end." A shiver runs through me, and I rub my arms. "I never want to endure that again, and no one should. And then there were the little green frogs."

Heads turn. Pairs of eyes are riveted to me.

Shawna says, "Frogs?"

I nod. "On assembly lines. But I set them free."

Ned claps her hands. "Enough chitchat. Let's get down to business."

"I've got to call my son," a woman says. "I lost my phone in the barn. Can I use yours?"

Another says, "My boss will be wondering where I am. Can I use your laptop and email her?"

"I need to call my mom," I say.

Chatter breaks out. Everyone has a request. We're all talking at once.

Ned raises her hand. "Listen up, everyone. I'm sorry, but I don't think you should contact anyone yet and tell them where you are. From what Miranda says, Chaos Biotech is sophisticated and may have a way to monitor my emails, calls, and texts."

Everyone groans.

Shawna says, "We're not in the barn, but we're being held captive."

Ned holds up a finger. "Just for a little longer. Hang in there with me, and we'll have a better chance of bringing down the people who did this to you. Now who wants to go first? Miranda, why don't you tell us your story. Then I'd like to know how the rest of you were locked in the barn together and what were you doing there."

When I tell Ned my story of what happened after I wandered into the barn, the others listen. Their mouths hang open. Ned records me on her phone and takes notes in a small spiral notebook.

"That's horrific," she says. "What an ordeal. Thanks for telling us about it."

I clench my fists and hope we're safe sitting here and not targets. What would we do if Martin Truex burst through the door?

"It was. I bet I'll have bad dreams about it for years. I'm glad we got out, instead of being held captive. But what about the secret facility for former employees on Cedar Island? We need to spring those people. They don't deserve to be imprisoned either."

Ned pats my hand. "We'll take one step at a time. We'll tackle the larger story first about Chaos and the Millersville operation, then move on to the detention center on Cedar Island. The authorities might be interested in the story and help free those people."

With a lump in my throat, I say, "My friend Natalie is in danger of being shipped off to the island. I wouldn't be a good friend if I didn't try to prevent that from happening to her. If I was in her situation, I'd want someone stepping up and protecting me in the name of justice."

"I hear you, Miranda," Ned says, "and we'll get to that later. Now, the rest of you, it's your turn. Who wants to go next?"

Shawna, my disc throwing partner, holds up her hand.

Ned points to her. "Go ahead."

"We're in a book club together, and we were meeting for coffee at Pelican Bay Bookstore in Millersville. We were going to discuss our latest book club pick, which it turned out was quite controversial due to charges brought against the author and her husband for an alleged crime overseas."

"I didn't like the book at all," a woman sniffs.

"Well, I loved it," another says. "It was atmospheric and set in a beach town. I really could feel like I was there."

Ned claps her hands. "Enough about the book. Right now, we're focusing on Chaos and their underhanded dealings. How did you end up in the barn?"

Shawna leans back against the couch. Those of us who aren't in chairs or on the sofa are sitting on the floor. I might've complained a week ago about getting a flat butt on the floor, but I'm safe and sheltered, so I hope, and grateful to be at Ned's place.

Shawna says, "We were on our way to the book shop, where they have excellent molasses cookies and cappuccinos, by the way."

A woman sitting on a folding metal chair says, "They are really good."

"Stick to the basics, please," Ned says, tapping her fingernails on a coffee mug. "We don't need to hear about food unless it's pertinent, or you were poisoned or drugged."

"Poisoned," a woman says, her eyes wide. "Can you believe it? It could've happened to us." She snaps her fingers. "We'd be dead, just like that."

"Ooh."

A hush fills the room, and I consider how close I came to dying. I could've been squeezed by a snake, drowned in filthy water, or fallen and broken my neck. Another instance flashes through my mind of when I evaded death. It could've been me, instead of Fiona, who died that day at summer camp. If she hadn't tried swimming, I might've hammed it up and shown off by diving in and doing backstrokes. I gulp.

A rush of gratitude fills me, and I realize that while I've been beating myself up for not saving Fiona, I could've been dragged in with her and drowned. I was young and not as strong as I am now. Although I couldn't pull her back to shore, at least I tried, which is more than the other girls in the river that day can say.

Looking around the room at the others, I'm proud of myself. I rammed a truck through the Chaos Biotech compound's front gate and saved these wonderful women. And what a story they've got to tell.

Shawna clears her throat. "So, we were about to get out of our cars, and we'd carpooled, because that's how we do things, when I got a text from an unknown number. It said my son was in trouble and needed help. It said for me and my friends to meet him at a barn on the edge of town."

I lean forward. "So, Chaos hacked into your phone and sent you the message?"

Ned holds up a hand. "Don't jump ahead and make assumptions. They could've obtained her phone number through a legitimate method. Keep going, Shawna. Tell us what happened next."

I glance at a cobweb hanging from the ceiling in a corner. I know all about falling for traps and giving out personal information to the wrong people. Like when I filled out the survey online to see if I was an orange or apple or a banana personality. I shake my head. I'll never do that again.

When I'm finished with diving into the details with Ned and fighting for what's right for those trapped as human subjects or sent away as former employees, I'll spend less time on social media. I was like a rat in a maze, searching for dopamine hits with each like.

Shawna says, "The text gave an address, so we rushed out to the property. When we couldn't find the place, instructions came by text. Look in the big barn, it said. So, we did."

"We found the barn and went in. Then the door slid shut, and they locked us in," a woman with defined cheekbones says. Although she's wearing a dirt-stained pink sweatshirt and matching sweatpants, she's glowing with health. I wish I was a natural beauty like that.

Shawna says, "We banged on the door and tried to

open the windows, but there were metal bars across them. We screamed, but no one came."

Ms. Pink workout outfit says, "We texted, we called, we emailed, but there was no cell reception." She runs her fingers through her precise bob cut, the type that looks like it was recently trimmed and falls against her neck just right.

I sigh with envy. For some people, looking good appears effortless. Maybe after this, I'll put in more of an effort, and floss my teeth twice a day. But I don't want to set the bar too high. Sweatpants or yoga pants are fine for me on all occasions.

I say, "There are ways to block cell reception, and they could've done that. They were monitoring you from a lab inside the underground facility, by the way. I saw it. People can watch what's going on in the barn."

Ned raises her eyebrows. "That's creepy."

We nod.

She stands. "Let's recap what we learned here today. You, Miranda, were trapped and treated like a subject in an experiment until you escaped."

"They called me Subject One," I say.

Shawna taps my shoulder. "I wouldn't take too much pride in that."

I flash her a smile. "Something about my past triggered their interest. They said they were studying the impact of trauma when you're young on adult development." I gaze at the group. "What about you? Did something happen before the age of say, fifteen, to change your life, and not in a good way?"

They're quiet. One by one, they nod.

"Maybe you were going to be next in their experiment," I say. "Subjects Two through Eleven."

Ms. Pink Outfit cringes. "But we didn't volunteer."

"I didn't either," I say with a shudder. "The cave, the frogs, the snake, the clown, the rising wastewater, and the gold discs. It was almost too much to take. We've got to stop them."

"And we will," Ned says with a gleam in her eyes. "Believe me, I'm all over this. Going back to your group, Shawna, you found yourselves trapped in that barn for how long, would you guess?"

She tilts her head. "Maybe ten hours or more?"

Ms. Pink Outfit says, "It felt like forever."

"It did," Shawna says.

"Give me your names, first and last, and where you live and email and phone numbers," Ned says. "Are each of you willing to go on the record about what happened to you? I'd like to quote you, if I could."

"Yes," we each say.

I say, "This can't happen to anyone else."

Shawna bites her lip. "Definitely, not."

Ned takes our information and taps her phone so it stops recording.

"I don't want to scare you, but I fear for your safety,"

she says. “Especially with cops possibly on the take and the security squad using metal-edged gold discs.”

“From what happened on the freeway,” I say, “and outside your building, I’d agree with that. We aren’t safe. They can find us.”

“We need to get you to a safe house, where you’ll be able to contact your families so they won’t worry. We need the communications to be private and protected. I don’t want Chaos knowing where you are until the story breaks.”

“Gosh,” Shawna says, “what’ll we do?”

Ms. Pink Outfit says, “Where will we go?”

“I have a friend who is a district attorney, and he knows people high up in the government,” Ned says. “Stay here, and I’ll call and see if I can get him in.”

She dials, and someone picks up on the other end.

“George, is this a good time? Sorry to call and not text first, but this is urgent.”

She listens and then says, “We need to speak in person, in a location that’s not compromised and unwanted ears can’t listen. I just ran a check for bugs, so we’re clear, at least for now. Can you come to my apartment?”

She knocks her knuckles on the wood windowsill, in a gesture I assume is for good luck.

“Alright, I’ll see you then. Make sure no one is tailing you. What I’m about to say is going to break a story wide open, and a certain business isn’t going to like it.”

25

We speak in hushed tones in Ned's living room. A half hour later, someone knocks on the door in what sounds like a code.

Knock. Knock. Knock. Tap, tap, tap.

Ned grins and flings the door open.

Mr. Red Robe thrusts out a hand, takes hers and shakes it.

"Martin Truex, may I come in?"

Ned's jaw is tense, but she steps aside.

He leans against a wall and acts casual, but I see him plant a small listening device by the door leading to the kitchen. I'll wait and see what he does before I take it and smash it to pieces. Better if it's there when he leaves, so he'll think he's outsmarted us. When people are relaxed and assume they've won, they make mistakes.

He looks around the room and locks eyes with me. I

stare back. I'm not intimidated. We're going to get him good and dish out what he deserves.

"Miranda," he says to me.

I say, "Martin, the flaming jackass. Why on earth do you wear a red robe? Because you have a king complex or something?"

He pulls the cape tight around his shoulders and glowers. The dark bags under his eyes are more pronounced than ever. His cold blue eyes could bore a hole into me.

"Young lady, watch your manners when you're addressing your superiors." He cackles. Turning to the others, he sprays spittle as he says, "And she thought she could outsmart me. But who is in charge now? Eh? Who came here to take Subject One away? She's going back with me."

He scans the room and points at the others. "And don't think you're going to home either. We must finish the study. We have a government grant and fixed time commitments. You're not getting out of this."

Sweat trickles down his face, and he wipes it away with his robe.

I bet that garment stinks, given how often he wears it, even in warm conditions.

I say, "You're a megalomaniac. You're obsessed with power, and you've lost touch with right and wrong."

The others nod.

"I'm upholding a fine well-honored, ethical tradition,"

he says in a booming voice. His cheeks are red and sweat flies from his face. "Scientists and businessmen everywhere envy me and what I've managed to accomplish in a short amount of time. No one has my net worth. I'm ranked at the top of the Forbes list." He gives us a crooked grin.

Ned turns to me and holds up a hand. "Don't say anything more. None of you. I don't want him to be able to use this against you."

He moves toward me, bearing down like a flatbed truck, and snakes out a hand, grabbing my wrist. "She's coming with me. And so are all the rest of you. My security squad is waiting on the street to pick you up. If you resist, I'll call them, and they'll haul you out of this simple apartment, just like that."

He leans down, putting his face far too close to mine.

I spit at him, temporarily blinding him, and twist out of his grasp, running to the door.

"All the better," he says. "She can't wait, and she wants to go back to Millerville and into our underground facility now. Isn't it right, dear Miranda?"

Ned walks up to him and pokes a finger at his chest. "Enough. My brother will be here soon. Leave, before I handcuff you in a citizen's arrest."

He laughs so loud, wine glasses in the kitchen ring.

Just then, there's a knock at the door.

"It must be my elite security squad," Martin Truex says with a smile. "Come in."

The door swings open.

In the doorway stands Frodo.

He's wearing a white shirt with a tie, a dark blazer, and gray pants.

"Frodo?" I say.

He gives me a grin. "George is my name in my work life."

Nodding to Ned, he says, "Hey, Sis, what's going on here?"

"This man is threatening us. His name is Martin Truex, and he owns Chaos Biotechnology."

George says, "Sir, come with me. We need to talk."

Martin Truex's eyes open wide. "My security team will be here any minute."

"They surrendered downstairs, and they won't be defending you. Now, will you come with me peacefully, or do we need to make arrangements that will be less comfortable?"

"I'll go," Martin says. "But money talks, and I have the best lawyers. They'll beat any charges you come up with." He swings toward me and points a long finger. "I'm not finished with you, Subject One. You're critical to the success of our company. We're not letting you go."

As a chill sweeps over me, I give him a hard squinting glare. Don't mess with me, mister. I've come through hell, and I won't put up with being held captive.

He leers at the others. "And that goes for the rest of you too. I'll be back."

Martin Truex gathers his red robe around him and stalks out the door, cackling.

Turning back, he says to me, "And don't try to free the fired employees on Cedar Island. We're about to transport them to a safer location. You'll never find them."

When the door closes, I rub my tight jaw. "Ned, you've got to nail this story and get this guy. Don't let us down."

"I won't," she says. "My brother is the best. He hates it when businesspeople care more about profit than human rights or regulations."

26

I chew on my lower lip in Ned's living room and think about what Martin Truex said about spiriting away his former employees from the secret detention center. I clear my throat. What I'm about to suggest to Ned is wild and reckless, but if we don't do it, no one will, and it'll be too late. The Feds will take too long. The people might be taken to another hidden location or killed. We'll never find the bodies.

I tug on Ned's arm to get her attention. She's talking to Shawna and getting a few more details about when they were held in the barn.

When she looks at me, I say, "We can't wait for your brother or anyone else to rescue those people on Cedar Island. We've got to go now and find them, before they're moved."

She sighs. "And here all I wanted was to write up the

story. But you're right. We can't leave them there. My brother and his team have their hands full now. He told me they don't have the staff to pursue the lead on the former employees. It could be weeks before they have time to look into it."

Shawna says, "We need to go. I'll join you."

"I will too," Ms. Pink Workout Outfit says.

"We'll all go," the others say. "With more of us, they can't hide."

"We'll outfox them," Shawna says with a smile. "Just try and stop us now."

Ms. Pink says, her fist in the air, "We are furious. We're a force to be reckoned with."

We all clap, and the hairs on the back of my arms stand on end. We may get this deed done with a dedicated group of warrior women.

Ned says, "You guys talk and make a plan while I write up my notes and send them to my editor."

"Wait," I say. "We forgot to sweep the area for bugs that Martin Truex might've planted. Don't say another word."

I fumble along the door jam, pull out a bug he planted, and smash it under my heel on the tiled kitchen floor. At the front door, I find another and crush it, venting my anger.

A knock at the door stops me. I look out the peep hole and see one of the middle-aged disc throwers from Chaos' security team.

"What do you want?" I say through the door.

"The rest of my team surrendered. I'm here to help you get to Cedar Island and rescue the fired employees from the detention center."

Turning to the others, I say, "Do you think we can trust her?"

Shawna shrugs.

Ned taps her lips.

Ms. Pink says, "We need the help. We don't know where to look, and I believe her."

Through the door, I say, "How did you know we were here and what we were planning?"

"That's easy. I was listening through the devices Martin planted in the apartment. Until you crushed them. Thanks a lot for that, by the way. My ears hurt from the crackling sound that came through when you smashed them."

I ask, "Is anyone with you?"

"No, just me, waiting at the door to help you go free innocent people who were locked up against their will. I've had a change of heart."

"I'll let her in," I say to the others, hoping I'm making the right choice.

She comes in and shakes my hand. "Subject One, it's an honor to meet you after you went through the gauntlet of tests they arranged. I'm Violet. Until an hour ago, I was head of Chaos's security."

Shaking her firm hand, I say, "What a relief it is to have you helping us. Let's make a plan and get going."

Ned types like a fiend and sends her article to her editor with the swoosh of a sent email. "Okay, that's done, for now at least. What are we doing, and when are we leaving?"

Violet checks her phone for the time. "If we don't leave in five minutes, it'll be too late. We've got to head up I-5 and hop on the ferry before it shuts down for the night. I'll take you to the detention center, which you wouldn't find without me guiding you. And then we'll make tracks and get off the island."

Shawna's eyes open wide. "Is it possible to do all that in a short amount of time?"

Violet nods. "It is, if you get your behinds in gear. Grab some water to drink and food to eat along the way, like granola bars."

"I've got those," Ned says. "And water bottles in my earthquake kit."

"Wear warm clothes and jackets, whatever you can find in the apartment. It may be cold where we're going, and we might have to cross the water on a boat at night."

I cringe because I'm not a fan of drama or death-defying stunts. I don't even rock climb. But I'm in for the rescue, despite it being out of my comfort zone.

"Do you know where my friend Natalie is? Did they take her to Cedar Island?"

Violet shakes her head. "They fired her an hour ago, and they're going to move her to the island in less than two hours. If we hurry, we might be able to catch her before she's admitted."

"Come on, guys," I say. "Find coats and sweaters. Let's get the food and water and go."

Pink says, "I have to stop in the bathroom first."

I wave my hands, making a shooing motion. "Then get going. We need to be out of here in less than five minutes. Natalie and the others on the island need our help."

"Who is going to drive?" Shawna says.

"I will," Ned says, raising her hand.

Violet says, "I have a minivan right outside."

As we pile into the two vehicles, with Ned and Violet driving, I hope we can trust Violet. Did she really switch sides, or is she here to gather information and point us in the wrong direction? Her transformation is a little too quick for me to buy it. I climb into Violet's van to keep an eye on her.

We head north on the freeway and drive west to Millersville, where we roll onto a 28-car ferry just as it is about to depart for Cedar Island. I'm hot in Ned's wool sweater and wind breaker, which are a size too small for me. I take long, slow breaths to calm my racing heart. We're going to the island. But can we pull off a rescue mission?

Crammed between Shawna and Ms. Pink, I drum my fingers on the seat.

Violet drives off the ferry onto Cedar Island and keeps going on a two-lane road straight ahead. She turns left at a sign for the Guemes Island Resort and bumps up a rutted dirt road. Ned follows close behind in her car.

Violet parks by a hedge and kills the engine, turning off the headlights. She points.

"You can't see it, but it's right over there. I can disarm the security system, but the guards are another matter. I may be able to talk them into surrendering. Do you have any cash? We could bribe them."

Looking at Shawna and Ms. Pink, I shrug. I don't have a phone, or my wallet or money. I left my belongings behind when I left Cabin Eight to take a walk in the woods.

"Nothing for me," I say.

"Same here," Ms. Pink says.

"I'll see if I can talk them into helping us," Violet says. "They're a dedicated group. I hired them for their valor and allegiance to a leader, not ethics."

My brow furrows. We're nobodies. We're not heroes. But then I think of the people being kept inside who are waiting to be rescued.

"We can do this," I say. "Come on, let's go."

When we tumble out of the van, I hold a finger to my lips. "Quiet."

Ned and her group join us.

"Ready?" Ned says.

"Ready," I say. "Let's get this done and get out of here."

27

Creeping up behind Violet, I smell her deodorant, the brand my mother wears. We crouch down behind a line of bushes. As my eyes adjust, I can make out a series of A-frame cabins in the woods. I'd expected a prison-like structure, but this looks like a holiday resort from the 1950s.

"There's a guard in each cabin," Violet whispers. "Former employees are held underground. We'll go through a cabin to enter a tunnel that leads to the cells."

I grimace. It seems impossible to get them out, but we've got to try.

"They're about to change guards," she says. "That's when we'll make our move."

A car pulls up, and tires crunch on gravel.

Two people get out.

Natalie says, "Is this the place? It doesn't look so bad. I'll just be here for a few days, right?"

"Time frame to be determined," a female guard says.

Leaves rustle.

Ned says in a low voice, "Is that your friend?"

I nod. "Yep."

She says, "Do you think we can get in there and free the others?"

"I'm not sure, what with the guards and a tunnel and underground holding cells."

She squeezes my hand. "I know. I have my doubts, but we've got to try."

My stomach growls, and I rest a hand on it. "It'll be tougher than I expected. This is where we show our grit and what we're made of."

"My brother would say that too. You'd be a good match."

"He's got a certain appeal," I say with a smile.

As the guard and Natalie approach us, Violet steps out of the bushes and walks toward them.

"Mimi, let her go. The rest of us surrendered. Martin Truex was taken in for questioning in Seattle."

Mimi grabs Natalie and holds her in a head lock.

Natalie makes choking noises and stares at me.

Mimi says, "I was hired to do a job, and I'm going to follow through. I'm no quitter. No one told me to knock it off. I'll wait right here and carry out orders until I hear from Martin Truex himself."

I let out a low whistle and go over to them with my hands up, so I won't appear threatening. "I don't mean any offense, but you sound like a zealot. It's over the top commitment to a cause when your boss here, Violet, tells you to stand down, but you refuse. Join our group. We're doing the right thing. We're going to free the fired employees."

Violet says, "It's over. The guards here don't know it yet."

"Well, shit," Mimi says. "I was saving for retirement. I just signed up for the 401k. What am I going to do for work now?"

Natalie pulls at Mimi's arm around her neck.

Violet goes over and pats Mimi on the back.

"I'll give you a recommendation and help you get a new job. Release her."

Mimi lets go of Natalie, who stumbles ahead, rubbing her throat.

"Miranda, is that you?" Natalie says. "What're you doing here?"

"Just enjoying the scenery," I say with a shrug. "I've always wanted to check out Cedar Island."

The others cock their heads and stare.

"No, not really," I say. "Just kidding. A group of us came here to rescue the people Chaos keeps here as prisoners."

Natalie's jaw drops open. "I heard it was a vacation place for employees who'd earned a sabbatical, with cabins by the shore and a to-die-for view. That's why I agreed to come along."

Furrowing my brows, I say, "The dying part might be spot on. Can you fill her in, Violet?"

Violet says, "This is not a place you want to voluntarily enter. Right now, there are nineteen former employees being housed in an underground bunker, below the A-frames. If you'd gone into a cabin, you would've been drugged by a guard and taken to a ten by ten-foot room with a barred window in the door. People don't escape, they die there. And the bodies are buried in a secret graveyard."

When she points to mounds in the forest about fifty paces away, I swallow hard.

Ned is writing in a small notebook. "How many are buried there?"

"More than you'd think," Violet says. "But now is not the time to discuss that. We need to disarm the guards and talk them into joining us."

My palms are cold. I wonder if what we're planning is possible.

"After we do that," I say, "what's the next step? How do we get into the underground tunnel? Do the cells have locks on them?"

Ned scribbles on her pad. "Yeah, how do we get down there?"

Ms. Pink whispers in my ear, "It's sounding dangerous, which is exciting. I'm in."

"Glad to hear that," I say. "We'll have to be brave."

Shawna says, "After what they did to me, I won't let that happen to anyone else."

Violet ticks off the answers to each of my questions on her fingers.

"One, there's a stairwell in each cabin leading down to the tunnel. Two, at the entrance to the tunnel is a one-foot-thick steel door. I have the key code and so does Mimi, but if we're incapacitated for some reason, the combination is..."

A gunshot goes off close by, and I jump.

It's close enough to scare us and loud enough to cover up Violet's answer.

"Duck hunters," Violet says. "Or it could be the islanders who oppose us. They've wanted to get us off the island for years."

My hands tremble. The situation is getting dangerous.

"Let's get this over with," I say. "Natalie, are you with us?"

"Just to be clear, my colleagues are in there? And they can't leave?"

Violet nods. "Affirmative."

"That's why I haven't heard from Jacques. Or Beth." She looks at me. "Yes, I'll help. What should I do?"

"Distract the guards." Ned tucks her notebook in a pocket. "We need someone to do that."

Violet says, "I think I should go in first and ask them to

leave. If they refuse, then we'll need a distraction. After that, we'll go inside and down into the tunnel."

"Right," I say, "it sounds like a plan."

My chest is tight, and my breathing is shallow. I'm ready to get this over with. I can't imagine how the scientists must feel, locked into cells when they thought they were going on a well-deserved sabbatical after toiling away in the underground laboratory.

Violet says, "Stay here. I'll be right back, I hope."

28

While Violet goes into the first A-frame, Natalie pulls me aside. "How did you get roped into this?"

"I wanted to help. After I was trapped in the barn and had to get through challenges where you worked, like climbing a wall and facing down a clown, I felt for the people imprisoned here. It's an injustice. We have to let them out."

She adjusts her glasses. "I can't I believe I fell for it. An all-expenses paid six-month sabbatical, starting with five nights at a rustic resort on Cedar Island."

"I fell through a trap door into a cave," I say, "so we're even."

Putting a hand to her head, Natalie says, "I believed in the research we were doing. I had no idea people were being held here."

Shawna steps forward. “And in the barns. They were going to do experiments on us.”

Natalie cringes. “We have a code of ethics. It’s supposed to be voluntary.”

Ned talks on her phone and says goodbye, pocketing her phone.

She says to me, “Introduce me to your friend.”

“Ned, this is Natalie, who worked at Chaos. Natalie, this is Ned. She’s a reporter for The Stranger in Seattle.”

Natalie shakes Ned’s hand. “I read your article about the mysterious building on South Lake Union.”

Ned chuckles. “The spooky steam plant piece came out just in time for the Halloween edition. I’d like to interview you. Do you have a minute?”

“Sure.”

Natalie and Ned walk away and stand talking while Ned records the interview.

Tiling my head, I look up at the dark sky. My thoughts are jumbled. My past and the present met up today when I talked about what happened at summer camp and saw Natalie and Ned. It’s almost too much. But I must be strong for a little longer, until we release the prisoners. Then I’ll collapse at my mom’s place and take a long, hot bath.

Violet comes out of an A-frame and strides over to us.

She’s smiling, so that’s a good sign.

“My guards agreed to lay down their arms and help us. I showed them a text about operations at Chaos being put on hold for the foreseeable future. Paychecks are suspended, so they decided they might as well help release the scientists who are held in captivity. The whole idea bothered them anyway. One guy said it was too much like Gitmo, but on American soil, and it was a violation of human rights. If we hadn't paid them so well, they'd have quit long ago."

I say, "Money mattered more than ethics, until now. We're going to right that wrong, and let the people go free."

Shawna sings, "Let my people go."

"Let's move," I say, heading toward the first A-frame. "Stay together."

The crack of a rifle stops me in my tracks.

Ms. Pink bumps into me.

A stocky man in camouflage pants and a matching jacket with hiking boots saunters toward us, gun in hand. His long gray beard comes to a point down on his chest.

"We're concerned community members, and we're here to shut this place down. Get in your cars and leave."

I put my hands on my hips. "You don't understand. We're here to rescue innocent people and set them free."

He says, "By a vote of the local islanders, this is now community-owned property. We're a sovereign nation and taking control. Get off the premises."

Violet and Mimi stride forward, cross their arms, and block his way.

I say, "Mr. Hunter of geese or ducks, or whatever you're

after, we're pursuing justice. Go back to the marsh, or wherever you came from. This is our land, and we have a job to do."

The man cups his hands and yells, "Hunters, hither!"

He pulls out a duck call and blows, making a quacking sound.

Out of the bushes step eight people wearing camouflage pants and jackets. They're carrying rifles and shotguns. They salute their leader and stand at attention.

With a frown, I wonder who they are, and what we're getting ourselves into. They look like they marched over from a quasi-military compound.

Natalie, Shawna, Ned, and Ms. Pink are whispering.

I wave my hands to get everyone's attention.

"You've interrupted a rescue mission. We'll go in and accomplish what we came here to do. Then you can do whatever you like. We'll be gone in no time."

The Leader steps forward and stands nose to nose with me.

He smells like cigars and whiskey.

"Listen here, young lady, we're not taking orders from you or anyone else. We have the authority to take over this compound. We don't like what's been going on here."

A woman in camo gear is chewing pink bubble gum.

She says, "It's time to put a stop to it. Too many cars and trucks roar down the road and don't stick to the speed limits. Bicyclists race around curves and go too fast.

People are dressed in guard uniforms, like it's Halloween every day out here."

The Leader nods. "Delivery trucks are putting ruts in our private road. But after today, no more of that. We're finished with being nice and negotiating."

He laughs, and the others join in.

A young man with a shaved head in his crew says, "We're taking back control."

I say, "What we've got is a disagreement about timing is all. What do you think, Violet? We'll be out of here in an hour?"

"Two hours, tops," she says. "And until I say so, you're not getting in. This is my facility, and I won't let you step foot on this soil until we're gone."

The Leader pokes Violet in the chest.

The gum chewing woman stands next to him.

"We'll decide what we'll do," he says. "And you won't order us around. Is that clear?"

Violet looks him in the eye. "No, it's not. I run this facility. You're breaking the law by standing here, trespassing. I'll report you. I'll get my guards to run you off."

"You will, huh?" he says. "I don't think so. You look too young to be running this place."

"That's right," the gum chewer says.

"Amen to that," says the young man with the shaved head. "Youth looks up to their elders, not the other way around."

"Some of us worked our way to the top," Violet says.

"Get off my land. Leave before I make a citizen's arrest and handcuff you all."

The leader spits on the dirt. "Not going to happen."

When he advances on her, she tugs on his beard, and he looks down.

Violet steps back and pulls out a gun.

Nine guns come up, aimed at our group.

Mimi, Violet's security officer, has her weapon out. She points it at the leader in camo gear.

Violet says, "Get off the property. Chaos Biotechnology owns it. And I swore to protect it."

"We'll be back," the leader says.

"That's right," the gum chewer says.

"Let's regroup," the leader says to his crew. "We'll get some food and consider the problem from all angles. It's a good training exercise."

As the group marches away, the young man in his twenties turns around and gives Violet the finger. "Take that!"

I shake my head. There's a lot of hatred in that bunch. I hope we're gone by the time they come back.

"Come on," Violet says, "let's go in and get out before they return with guns blazing the next time."

29

As we approach the first A-frame, a guard comes out and stands on the front porch.

He's big and broad-shouldered. His bulging biceps poke out of a yellow Chaos t-shirt. From the way he stands tall, he looks like he's ex-military, and he likes to work out.

"You sure about this?" he says to Violet. "The operation is definitely shut down?"

"I am," she says.

He wipes his eyes with the back of a hand. "We've got a baby on the way. We were about to buy a house. I need that paycheck."

Violet says, "Let's do the right thing for these former employees and worry about the paycheck later. We'll talk."

He rubs his chin. "I need more than talk. I need a

salary with benefits and medical insurance. My wife is on bed rest. She can't get a job."

Violet pats his arm. "Come on, Vincent. Tomorrow I'll form a security company and hire you all. I promise, your family won't starve, and that baby will be taken care of."

He nods. "Okay, thanks. What'll we do next?"

"We're going in," I say, "and we'll let the people go free. But how will we transport them off the island? We should've thought of that before this, I guess."

We look around the group.

Violet says, "No Lyft or Uber out here. It's too rural."

The guard says, "The ferry is down for the night."

Ned holds up an index finger. "I'll make a few calls. Go ahead, I'll be right behind you. I don't want to miss seeing that tunnel in person and how the employees react."

Violet says, "Vincent, gather the other guards and serve as lookouts. Let me know if anyone shows up who is unwanted. We ran into a group just now that looked like a quasi-militia. Keep an eye out, and don't let them inside. They're armed and dangerous, and they want to take over the compound."

While Vincent goes off to talk to the other guards, we huddle together on the front porch.

Violet says, "Here's the plan. I'll go first, then Miranda and Shawna and the others. Mimi will cover our tail. And Ms. Pink there, if we end up in gunfire, take off that pink sweatshirt, or you'll be a target. Here we go. Operation Freedom for Former Chaos Employees is now in motion."

Ned runs up and joins us just as we go into a cabin.

Inside, the A-frame looks like any other vacation cabin. Wood panel on the walls. A braided rug on the floor. River stones surround a wood-burning fireplace with a deep hearth. The room smells of wood smoke.

Off to the left is a kitchen area with a counter, a sink, and a two-burner stove.

The white frig is ancient and emitting a humming noise.

"This way," Violet says. She unlocks a door in the hall next to the bedroom and opens it. She flicks on a light. "Down we go."

Tramping down wood steps, I hold onto a handrail.

We've got a good plan, but so much could go wrong. The group with guns might shoot us and leave the employees locked up. We don't have transportation out of here for all of us. I hope Ned worked something out.

Ahead is a wide tunnel with lights in the wall every few feet.

"Cool," Ms. Pink says.

"It is," I say.

It's a wonder the company built this underground, and it's cold down here. But we'll only be down here a few minutes, so I can tolerate it. What would it be like to be locked up here?

We stop at a steel door. The metal skin shines, reflecting light. It almost has a halo. Good things aren't happening below ground here. We're walking into evil resulting from a crazed mad man.

"And now for the combination," Violet says.

Gunshots ring out in the distance.

Footsteps pound down the stairs.

"Stop right there," says the Leader. "You've entered hallowed ground. Go back."

Ignoring him, Violet punches in the key code.

The foot-thick door swings open.

She says, "You don't scare us."

She may be confident, but my hands are shaking as I move past the massive door.

The leader tries to stride ahead, pushing past us, but we block him.

Mimi pulls out a plastic zip tie and handcuffs him behind his back before he can protest. He squawks and swears.

Mimi says, "Stay out of the picture while we get the job done."

"Dang it," he says. "What the heck do you think you're doing? Where's my militia? They were supposed to be right behind me."

Mimi says, "They might've been delayed. We have lookouts, and they're trained killers. You don't want to mess with us."

"Help," a woman cries from a cell. She's holding onto the bars. Tears are streaming down her cheeks. "Are you here to save us?"

"We are," Violet says. "Your security team had a change of heart. Martin Truex is being questioned. You're free to go."

She unlocks each of the cells.

A man with a grizzled salt and pepper beard hugs her. His clothes are rags, hanging off his thin frame. "Thank you. It's been so long. I'd given up hope."

"Never give up hope," Shawna says. "We were stuck in a barn until Miranda let us out. We thought we'd be in there forever."

The freed former employees are haggard. Their faces are gray and lined with wrinkles. Dark smudges under their eyes indicate they haven't had much sleep.

I say, "Let's go topsides and find a way to get you off this island."

"I've got that covered," Ned says with a smile.

"What did you arrange?"

"You'll see. It'll be better if it's a surprise."

As we file out, the Leader shouts, "What about me? You can't leave me in here."

Mimi says with a shrug, "I handcuffed him in a cell. He was a pain in the ass."

"Help," he says.

"We'll send in the authorities to get him after we're settled," Mimi says. "Gives us leverage if his group gives us trouble."

"Love that door," Ned says, taking a photo with her phone.

She snaps a few more pictures, and we take the stairs, following the freed prisoners, who are shaky on their feet. They are pulling themselves up by the handrail, and it looks like an effort.

On the front porch, we stop and survey the property.

Chaos guards have tied members of the leader's militia to trees and taken their guns.

"Cut us loose," the gum chewing woman yells.

"I didn't sign up for this harassment," the young man with the shaved head says with a snarl. "Cut the bullshit and let us go."

"Ned, how are we getting out of here?" I say.

She points to the sky. "That's our way out."

30

A helicopter appears in the jet-black night sky and flies toward us. It hovers over a clearing by the road. Rotor blades thump.

When the helicopter sets down, we let out a cheer.

"How'd you arrange that?" I say to Ned.

She shrugs. "If you've got pull, you use it."

"But we can't all fit in there."

Violet pulls out her phone. "Get as many of the prisoners in there and take off. I'll arrange for other transportation off the island."

"Tom," Violet says. "Are you still at work and ready to fly?"

She listens. "Good, I need you to bring the yellow bird. Touch down at the Cedar Island facility as soon as possible. We need transport to Millersville. The ferry is down for the night, and we've got a load of people to get the heck off this island before the locals hunt us down."

She hangs up and pockets her phone.

"All set," she says to us. "That's taken care of. He'll be here soon."

To Ned, she says, "Have the helicopter pilot take the first group of people to a triage center outside of Millersville. Land by the Chaos Biotech transit shed on the outskirts of town. They'll need food and water and medical care."

"And I need to debrief them," Ned says, "as does my brother."

When the pilot takes off with the first load of passengers who were imprisoned below the A-frames, we wave.

Watching it fly away toward Cedar Channel, I hope we won't be stranded here all night. The thought of it makes me shudder. The facility gives me the creeps.

"We've got to get out of here," I say. A wave of dizziness washes over me, and I bend over to clear my head.

"Hey," Violet says, resting a hand on my arm. "Don't worry, we've got this handled. Just a little longer, then this will all be over."

A breeze picks up, brushing past my cheeks. Taking a slow breath to calm myself, I smell salt air mixed with sulfur from guns being fired. Maybe, with the help of my new friends, everything will work out, and we'll be sleep in a safe place tonight.

A massive yellow helicopter with the Chaos corporate

logo, which is a capital C with a circle around it, hovers before setting down in the clearing.

"That's our UH-1 Iroquois, otherwise known as the Huey," Violet says with a smile. "It'll hold all of us."

"Are we taking the island militia members?" I say, looking at them squirm, tied to trees.

"Nope, we'll leave them here," Violet says. "We've got enough to deal with for now. I'll call it into the Millersville police. They can take care of it."

"We should do something," Shawna says. "They threatened us with firearms."

Mimi cocks her head. "They're allowed to carry guns. They'd probably say they were duck hunting when the gun went off. Lots of duck hunting on the island."

We pile into the huge helicopter, and there's room for all of us. Mimi and the other Chaos prison guards pat each other on the back and talk in loud voices about working for Violet when she starts a new security company.

Shawna and Ms. Pink's book group who were trapped in the big barn lean against each other and hold hands. Despite all they went through, they're smiling, and they have color in their cheeks. I bet they've never felt so alive.

That's true for me too. My chest is light, and I sigh as a feeling of accomplishment fills me. I lean back, sitting between Ned, who is writing in her notebook, and Violet, who is texting with quick thumb movements on her phone.

When the helicopter lifts off, we all cheer, and I yell the loudest.

Pumping my fists in the air, I shout, "We're free. We're safe. We did it!"

Ten minutes later, we touch down.

When the rotors stop moving, we hop out and look around.

The land is flat and bare. No trees are growing here. A white one-story building sprawls across the grounds. Next door, there's an airplane hangar. Twenty white unmarked vans are lined up in rows in a fenced yard.

Violet says to the pilot, "Thanks, I'll take it from here."

In a loud voice, she says to the group of us standing there, "This is our transit shed, where we can get warm and eat food. I'm sure many of you are dehydrated, so be sure to drink water. We have a disaster-preparedness cache of food here and a complete set up with sleeping bags and cots in case of an earthquake. Mimi and I and the guards will set up food tables and get you served, then we'll talk about sleeping arrangements."

Ms. Pink raises her hand. "Our book group members live about fifteen miles away from here. Can we go home?"

"I'd rather you didn't," Violet says. "Of course, we can't keep you here against your will, but it's late, you're exhausted, and you've all been through a traumatic situation. We'd like to debrief you and provide you with support services. We have counsellors on call who can come in on a moment's notice. You'll find a debrief session will help you decompress. You had a shared experience filled with grief, and it may help to talk about it."

Ned nods, standing with her pen poised above her notepad, eyeing the others. "It's almost impossible to find a therapist these days. I've been on a wait list for months. You might want to take advantage of the opportunity."

"We'll provide phones," Mimi says, "so you can contact your loved ones and tell them where you are."

Natalie links arms with two haggard, imprisoned scientists and they walk into the building through huge sliding doors.

Ms. Pink says to her friends, "I'm exhausted. What they're proposing sounds good, just for tonight. We'll go home tomorrow."

Violet motions to the white building. "Come on, then, let's go inside and get warm and some food in your bellies. I promise you we won't keep you here against your will. You are free to go."

Turning to Mimi, Violet says, "Text the counsellors and get them on site ASAP. This is an urgent, one-off situation."

Just then, Natalie's brother pulls up in his white van.

Frodo hops out, as do three others carrying briefcases.

When they hustle over to us, Frodo says to me, "You okay?"

I grin. "Never better. I've made peace with my past. We served justice, and we're on the other side of chaos. It's all downhill from here."

31

The next day, newspaper headlines read, "Scandal uncovered at Chaos Biotechnology. Regulatory violations revealed. Secret government contract revealed."

I'm interviewed by radio and television stations. For once, I'm comfortable in my own skin, looking right at the reporters asking questions and knowing I did something amazing. I managed to right a tremendous wrong.

My mother is mad at me for not calling her first thing from Ned's place. She broke down in tears when I called her from the transit center. She loved the story of how I drove a truck through the chain link fence and freed the book club women in the barn.

Sandy's Produce found their truck at the rest stop, where we left it. Sandy said given the circumstances, she'd let it go and not press charges. It was a life and death situation, and her truck saved us. She said her insurance will pay for the damages.

Ned's story ran in all the news wire services. She was offered jobs in New York and LA, but she told me she wants to stay in Seattle. Family is more important, and George is here for now. She says there's more dirt under the rug she can uncover in the local area, and she's got a new lead about a missing item in Millersville.

Frodo and I met for coffee. We've got a date to walk around Green Lake next week, so I'll see what happens. I'm fine either way.

Most important of all, I tracked down the former motel owners and called them to meet, so I could apologize in person.

Driving to their place, I gripped the steering wheel tight. I'd gone back to the Two Rivers Resort to get my car and stuff from Cabin Eight. Before I left, I picked up the red mitten on the floor and tucked it in a trash can outside. I wheeled the little red tricycle outside and left it by the motel office.

Knocking on the door of the motel owners, my gut churns. It's time to face up to what I did and apologize. I'd taken the couple's way to make a living from them.

"Hello, I'm Miranda."

The middle-aged owners stand side by side with rigid posture. They don't invite me in, and I don't deserve their courtesy or kindness.

I clear my throat, and wring my hands, forcing out the

words. "I wanted to say I'm sorry I broke the rules and burned the pages of my diary in your motel. I've never apologized directly to you, and I should have."

Tears stream down the man's cheeks.

The woman hides her face in her hands, and she weeps.

She says, "We've been waiting to hear you say that. Come in. I've got a pot of coffee going."

When we're sitting at their kitchen table, she says, "Did it help you heal from the past? By burning the pages with your writing on it?"

I cock my head, considering. "I thought it would, but after the fire, more guilt piled on. I've been carrying it around since I burned you out of your business."

Pulling a check out of my purse, I push it across the table. "This is the extent of my savings, and I want to give it to you. It isn't much, but I want you to have it. I'll send more with the reparation payments. I won't ever be able to make it up to you, but I'm going to try my best. Again, I'm so sorry. And thank you for agreeing to see me. I should've done this long ago and not waited so long."

They stare at the check for three thousand dollars and look at me with watery eyes.

She says, "We can't accept this. You're young and getting started. We shouldn't deplete your savings. You might need it."

He slides the check so it's in front of him.

"Actually," he says," we could use this. We've had some

medical bills mounting, and we need to pay them. This is a lifesaver, just when we needed it."

She nods. "You're right."

Turning to me, she says, "Thank you. This is a timely gift, and we appreciate it."

I drove home that evening, feeling better about myself. I'm acting like an adult.

That night, I reached out to Fiona's parents to tell them I had information about how their daughter died. They weren't home, so I left a message.

Fiona's mom called back five minutes later. "What do you have to tell me about my daughter's death?"

Holding the phone with sweaty hands, I say, "I was with your daughter when she passed away at camp. She went swimming in the river, but the current carried her away. I tried to grab her, but I couldn't. I'm so sorry about her death."

She's quiet for a moment, and I hear sniffling.

She blows her nose. "Why was she in the deep part of the river in the first place? I never heard about that."

With a lump in my throat, I say, "She said she wanted to swim. She was showing us the breaststroke before she was swept away."

"Can you tell me more about what happened? I've always wondered, especially late at night when I can't sleep."

"She looked really happy, like she was having the best time of her life when she dove in. She was always doing crazy things, like jumping off the dock in choppy water or climbing too high in a tree. The counsellors would scold her, but this time she was too fast for them to do anything about it. She was suddenly swimming, and we couldn't stop her."

Fiona's mom sighs. "She always was a risk taker and testing her limits. It was a trial at times, taking her to the emergency room for a broken wrist or a sprained ankle. But what a joy she was. I've never met anyone like her."

Goosebumps cover my flesh. "I haven't met anyone like Fi ever. I miss her every day. Her joy was contagious."

I wipe away tears.

"Now don't you go blaming yourself for not saving my daughter. She was the one who went in the deep water. She risked her life. You were young, and you did your best. I don't want you to carry around this guilt for the rest of your life. It's not your burden. It's mine." She pauses. "Or maybe it's no one's. Let's agree to move on from this moment and leave our guilt behind. Do you agree?"

I take a deep breath. "Yes, I agree. I'll set it down and leave it behind."

"Good, now get some sleep and live your best life for your friend Fiona. Do everything you want to do in the mightiest, most fierce way you can, in my daughter's honor. And thank you for calling. Maybe we can both get some shut eye tonight."

"Thank you. Good night."

Hanging up, I set down the phone and blow my nose.

I'm free from the past mistakes I've carried for too long. It's time to live my life and focus on the here and now.

I pace the room. The motel owners need money. What can I do to pay reparations to them with more money every month?

I stop and taps my lips. I could move in with my mother to save money. She says I can come back and live in my childhood bedroom. Although I'd rather live by myself, it's time to step up and own what I did and be responsible for the fire.

I nod. I'll let go of my apartment, save money, and work extra shifts on my house-cleaning job. It'll take a long time to pay off my debt, but if I can rescue women in a barn before they were subjected to experiments and help free former Chaos employees, I'm up for this.

Crossing my arms, I grin. I'll go seventy in a forty mile an hour zone. It'll take time, but I'll increase the reparation payments and make it right for the motel owners. When we met, they mentioned their insurance would cover re-building the damaged rooms, so I hope they'll reopen the motel.

Chaos Biotechnology is undergoing upheaval. Martin Truex has been charged with kidnapping and regulatory violations. Frodo, or George, says they're building an airtight case against him.

Ms. Goggles and Beverly and Piper have been in touch. They're going to start a company to research life-saving treatments. This time, they won't trap human subjects for experiments. It'll be above board and ethical, they assured me.

Violet opened a security firm and hired her staff, including the middle-aged female disc throwers. The last time we met for coffee, she was grinning from ear to ear, so I guess it's going well. Two high-tech businesses signed contracts for her company's services in the first week, so she's busy.

I pull out a cardboard box and load my diaries and candles inside, along with books I'll be taking with me to my mother's place. I toss in my clean Chaos sweatshirt and pants, which I'm keeping as a souvenir of my time in captivity. The vivid canary color reminds me to not dwell on the past. And, if the situation calls for it, to step up, be a hero and rescue those in need.

It's not all about me anymore.

Other lives are important, and if I can help, I will.

One thing I know is I won't be burning pages from my diary inside ever again.

I've learned my lesson.

Reader questions:

1. Did you think it was realistic for a company to gather information from Miranda's social media activity and her answers to an online

survey? How, if at all, might reading this book change your online behavior going forward?

2. Did you root for Miranda early in the book? Or, did you dislike her and blame her because she started a fire and entered an off-limits barn?
3. When Miranda was trapped in the underground facility, did you think she was going to be able to escape? What would you have done if you were in her situation?
4. Would you have run for home at the end or rescue the others? Why or why not?
5. What was the most exciting part of the book for you?
6. What did you think of how Miranda made amends at the end of the book with the motel owners? Would you have handled it in a different way?
7. Do you think a company might skirt laws and regulations in the pursuit of profit? How were Chaos employees complicit? If you worked there, would you have reported the company to regulatory authorities or stayed silent?
8. Miranda faces several fears throughout the book. Do you feel she had to do that as a punishment for her wrongdoings or was there another reason? Have you ever had a moment

where you've had to face your fears? Was that a cathartic process?

Thanks for reading this! Please let other readers know what to expect by posting reviews on Goodreads, Amazon and Bookbub.

Want to know what happens to Violet? Read my next book,
The Mother's Threat to watch your back today!

If you enjoyed Cabin Eight, then sign up here for my newsletter to be the first to hear about my other books.

Find me on my Facebook author page
Follow me on BookBub for the latest updates!

ACKNOWLEDGMENTS

I'm deeply grateful to Sue Toth for her developmental editor insights. A huge thanks to Rick Dahms of Rick Dahms Photography for a professional headshot. Thanks to Bill Isenberger at Axis Studios in Seattle for his website expertise for: www.susanspechtoram.com.

Thanks to the Pacific Northwest Writers' Association. Many thanks to the Women's Fiction Writers Association for support and information. Most of all, thank you to my parents, Liz and Ed, to my children, Nick and Forrest, and to my husband Jerry, for making me laugh.

ABOUT THE AUTHOR

Susan is writing mysteries, thrillers, and suspense novels. Previously, she served as senior director of corporate communications for biotechnology companies. Susan worked as an activity aide in an upscale nursing home's psychiatric unit. She was a potter and painter with an art studio in Seattle and has also been a market researcher, a nurse's aide, and a waitress. Her essays have been published in Mothering Magazine, Twins Magazine and Utne Reader.

Susan grew up near Detroit, Michigan and received a BFA with Honors from University of Oregon and an MBA in Marketing from Seattle University. She lives in a windy part of the Pacific Northwest with her husband and rescue dog.

BOOKS BY SUSAN SPECHT ORAM

Shore Lodge, a high-stakes psychological thriller

The Thieves, a high-stakes entertaining heist thriller

Cabin Eight, a speculative psychological thriller

The Mother's Threat, a compelling domestic thriller

Secrets at the Cafe, a novel of suspense about family and friendship

Humorous fiction:

Boating with Buddy, a report from a canine correspondent

Nonfiction:

Brief business books on investor relations, crisis communication and public relations

Made in the USA
Las Vegas, NV
28 February 2024

86466838R00134